SLIP AND SLIDE

By G B Ralph

The Rise and Shine series
Duck and Dive
Slip and Slide
Over and Out

SLIP AND SLIDE
Rise and Shine – Book Two

G B RALPH

Copyright © G B Ralph 2020

This book is copyright. Apart from any fair dealing for the purpose of private study, research, criticism or review, as permitted under the Copyright Act, no part may be reproduced by any process without permission of the publisher. The moral rights of the author have been asserted.

ISBN 978-0-473-59072-7 (Paperback POD)
ISBN 978-0-473-59073-4 (Epub)
ISBN 978-0-473-59074-1 (Kindle)

A catalogue record for this book is available from the National Library of New Zealand.

G B Ralph
www.gbralph.com

For Buddha, Snowball, and Barclay,
for keeping us sane during lockdown.

Chapter 1
We love him though, don't we?

'Come on, Theo! What are you doing in there?' I said, knocking on the bathroom door.

'I am *trying* to have a nice, relaxing bath,' he said through the door. 'And your banging is devastating to my chill, so beat it.'

Claire wandered past, taking a bite from her toast. 'What's the bet that skinny, white boy is beating something else in there,' she said, winking as she headed from the kitchen into the living room. 'He'll be luxuriating in a nice, long wan—'

'Yes, got it. Ew,' I said. 'But... you're probably right.'

'I'm right, Gabriel,' Claire said as she stepped over the neighbour's cat – Betty – and skirted around the easel and half-formed sculptures. The moment she dropped onto the couch, Betty hopped up next to her.

'First: why must he do it in our *shared* bathroom? And second: why *right now*? I've got my shift this morning,' I said, then turned to cast my voice through the closed door, 'like I do *every week*.'

'You know our Theo – our resident whirlwind of obliviousness – do you really think he's aware what day it is?' Claire said, idly patting the cat. After sipping her tea, she cleared her throat and raised her voice. 'Theo. Stop jerking off and let Gramps in, he's got work.'

The reaction was immediate. 'Sorry, Claire! I'll be out in a minute,' he said, coupled with sounds of water sloshing about and things crashing to the floor.

'Why does he listen to you?'

'He may be too wrapped up in his own world to consider most anyone else… but he's infatuated with me,' she said, 'obviously.'

'What? No, he's not.' I turned from the bathroom to focus on Claire, serene as ever, eating her breakfast under Betty's watchful eye. We never fed the cats, only put out water for them, but they were ever hopeful.

I noticed Basil then too, the neighbour's other cat. The lump of ginger fur napping in his usual corner spot, high on the couch back. From his perch, Basil could survey the room – like a king on his throne, deigning to grant his subjects an audience with their monarch. Provided the peasants remained at arm's length with no undignified touching.

'Look at Theo's paintings and sculptures,' Claire said, gesturing to the numerous pieces of art scattered around our living room. The works were at varying stages of incompleteness, the product of frantic and feverish all-nighters. Jugs of instant coffee, microwave pizza, and pot noodles sustained his efforts, inevitably followed by two days crashed on his bed.

'So,' she said, 'do you notice anything?'

'They're all half-baked and making a mess of our living room?' The only time I ever looked was when I needed to shuffle something aside to clear a path, or adjust a dropcloth to catch any paint splotches. 'I've never considered Theo's art, not properly.'

'Well, not really your favoured subject matter, is it?' Claire said.

I looked now, really looked. 'There *are* a lot of breasts, aren't there?'

'Yes, well, he is a rather sexually repressed straight boy, so…'

'And his subjects, they all have dark skin. Dark, curly hair…' I looked to Claire, to Theo's art, then back to my flatmate again. 'They're all *you*.'

Claire clapped, though it was more sarcastic than triumphant.

I scowled. 'I hadn't noticed.'

'Age really doesn't equal wisdom, does it?'

'Hey, I'm only a few years older than you two.'

'More like six or seven years, old man.'

Unlike Theo, Claire was smart, focused, organised. A science student, majoring in geology – a solid degree. And mature beyond her years, Claire was unnervingly perceptive. Without me saying a word, she knew I was struggling in this new city, away from everyone and everything I knew.

Theo burst from the bathroom then, towel wrapped around his skinny waist, and wet hair covering half of his face like a raggedy old mop. At least he'd washed it for once. 'Sorry, Claire. Didn't realise you were up already.'

'Free cardio class at the Rec Centre this morning, isn't it?' Claire said. She too had a lot of hair, but it always looked good – Claire made everything look effortless.

'Oh, yeah. Right, of course,' Theo said, still standing in the doorway in his towel. Was he... was he posing? Claire was so right.

'What am I, chopped liver?' I said, still waiting for the bathroom.

'Uh? What *are* you talking about?' Theo said, turning to face me with his habitual look of incomprehension.

'Never mind, get out,' I said, shooing him away.

'All right, Gramps,' Theo said, relaxing his pose and stepping aside. These two really made me feel like a grumpy old prick sometimes.

I'd finally made it into the bathroom and slammed the door behind me. It'd have to be a quick turnaround if I wasn't going to be late. In my haste to get the shower going, I slipped on the puddles of water Theo had left. I grabbed a hold of the tap, saving myself from crashing to the floor.

I took a breath, pulled myself to vertical and turned on the shower. There was a wobble in the tap I'm sure wasn't there before, but it was working fine now – I'd have to keep an eye on it.

I shed my clothes and stepped under the stream of hot water over the bath tub.

They were all right, really – my flatmates. It was good to have people around when I got home.

Having worked straight out of school and now starting university at 26 years old, I was considered a 'mature student'. Surrounded by teens and early twenty-somethings every day, I was an oddity, a curiosity, but one that most seemed unwilling to investigate too closely. I'd had trouble meeting people my own age because they were all working, living their adult lives, like I should be. I was stuck in some kind of social limbo. To be fair, I had met some people, but the friendships didn't extend beyond class. And I'd even met a guy – that went well... until it didn't. But we don't talk about that.

Anyway... Claire, Theo and I were an odd trio, but we'd met at the flat viewing and seemed willing to take a punt on each other and the flat. We signed up on the spot. The cheap rent was the clincher – it meant I only had to pick up a few shifts at the driving range each week. And working there doubled as an opportunity to meet people too – I was ever hopeful.

I finished my shower and changed into my uniform. This was cutting it fine, but I still ought to make it to work on time. I threw my book, drink bottle and lunch into my backpack, and headed for the front door.

I almost had it open when I caught a whiff of the mat.

'Fuck's sake, Basil!'

'What? What's happened?' Claire said, stalking out of her bedroom. 'He's asleep on his perch.'

'Pissed on the door mat again, hasn't he?' I said.

'Sneaky little bastard,' Claire said.

I considered leaving it to the others to sort out, but decided against it. Picking up the soiled mat by the corners, I carried it through the flat – trying to avoid inhaling the acrid stench – dropped it into the bathtub and rinsed it off.

'When you gotta go, you gotta go,' Theo said.

I turned to see my flatmate nodding sagely from the bathroom doorway, wearing the same Pikachu top as yesterday. 'Theo... did you change back into the same clothes?'

'Yeah, I didn't spill anything on myself all day yesterday,' Theo said, pulling the hem of his top to show me, looking rather proud of himself. 'So, he's good for another round.'

'You – No. No, I don't have time,' I said, deciding it wasn't worth it.

'Basil is getting on, you know...' Claire said, joining Theo outside the bathroom to watch me wash the mat. 'At least he did it on the mat, right?'

I sighed. 'Yeah. But we'd better watch him when he's in the house.' It was the third time he'd done it this month, but none of us could bring ourselves to lock the little piss-bag out – he was too adorable.

I turned off the water and hung the mat over the towel rail to dry.

'Gabriel, are you off soon?' Claire said.

'Yeah, now. Why?'

'Can you take the rubbish out?'

'I've really got to go, Claire,' I said, trying to get past my flatmates loitering in the doorway.

'It'll only take a sec. It's ready to go – I've tied up the bag in the kitchen.'

'Sure. Yes, OK.' It would be quicker to just do it. I dashed into the kitchen, grabbed the black bag and—

Exposed a pool of sticky liquid on the floor. It reeked almost as bad as the door mat.

'Bin juice!' I investigated the bottom of the black bag to find a neat claw mark with food scraps hanging out, but no cat in sight.

Claire appeared in the kitchen. 'Basil's on form this morning...'

'He's not even our bloody cat.'

'We love him though, don't we? Don't worry Gabriel, I'll clean it up, you go,' she said, waving me out of the flat.

I didn't need any more encouragement so made my escape before I was interrupted again, careful to hold up the bag by the tear to avoid more drippage.

The driving range wasn't far away, but I'd really have to get moving to avoid being late. Not that I'd get my pay docked or anything like that – but my boss, Murray, would *pass comment*. Something passive aggressive about the clock being out because he'd expected me a few minutes ago. Or he'd feign ignorance of the roster, like he didn't know precisely when I should be there. And then I'd have to endure low-key digs all morning about time management and reliability and 'early is on time, on time is late' and yadda yadda yadda. It was not worth it.

The apartment building door swung shut as I dropped the rubbish bag over the railing and stormed down the front steps.

I'd almost made it to the footpath when I heard a shrill call from behind me. 'Mr Bedford!'

My step faltered. I briefly considered pretending I hadn't heard – though, with no headphones on, and the volume and pitch of that screech, no one would believe such a feeble excuse. I'd pay for it later if I didn't turn around.

'Yes, Mrs Sheffield?'

May I introduce our landlady, Sharon Sheffield. She owned and lived in the apartment directly beneath the one we rented from her. We took a perverse pleasure in dropping our rubbish bags on the pile beneath her window – the building's designated drop-off point. With such a sight and smell, Sharon was forced to keep her kitchen windows and blinds closed.

'Ah, young man, I'm glad to have caught you. Are you heading out?' she said, calling from her front patio around from the front steps.

'Yes, Mrs Sheffield, I'm off to work,' I said, trying to edge away.

'You're a good boy, aren't you? So hard-working, and all while studying full time. Polite too, not like the young people in my other properties.'

I took a breath to halt the snide responses on the tip of my tongue. 'Thank you, Mrs Sheffield—'

'Now, you must call me Sharon, young man. I insist,' she said, chuckling to herself. '"Mrs Sheffield" makes me sound so old, I'm no matron yet.'

Who was she kidding?

'Now, that's pronounced Sha-RON, mind you, emphasis on the second syllable. Have I told you about the origins of my name?'

'Actually, yes—'

'It's Hebrew and means "the valley". It's also the name of the rose of Sharon that Jesus plucked on his way to Galilee. "I am the rose of Sharon, the lily of the valley." That's from the King James translation of the Song of Solomon. Isn't it wonderful?'

'Indeed it is, Sharon. But I really must get to—'

'Yes, yes, of course. I was just calling out because I wanted to remind you about the Residents Committee meeting this week. As Chairperson I highly encourage attendance by all residents – both property owners like me and tenants such as yourself – we haven't had representation from you or the other two for months now.'

Our landlady took on the role of Residents Committee Chairperson a few years ago, having run unopposed. And so, emboldened by her victory, the first item on her agenda was relocating the rubbish pile.

'Mm, yes, we've all been very busy,' I said, attempting to edge away again.

'Of course, of course. But the rubbish issue – front of mind for many residents – is on the agenda again this week. We last discussed it six months ago, and I believe it's time to reconsider, especially with the warmer weather strengthening the uh… the aroma. It would be a real help to have your support at the meeting.'

That mound of stinking black bags wouldn't be going anywhere – not when it was already so convenient for everyone else, and more importantly, not outside their windows.

I gave no response, so she continued, 'It's on Wednesday evening, 7pm.'

'Oh, that's unfortunate,' I said, a blatant lie. 'I have the evening shift at the driving range on Wednesday so won't be able to attend.' That was true. 'I'll send Theo or Claire in my stead.' Another lie, there was zero chance they'd show.

Sharon pursed her lips at the suggestion. 'Are you sure you won't be available?'

'No, sorry. I've already committed to the shift, can't let my boss down,' I said, playing the responsible young person card, then followed up with the fatal blow. 'And I've got to keep the shifts up, make sure I can keep paying the rent on time.'

'Yes, good boy. Very responsible,' Sharon said, nodding. 'Well, I'd better let you get to work.'

'Have a good day, Mrs – Sharon,' I said, careful to emphasise the second syllable, then turned to go.

'Oh, Mr Bedford. One more thing: have you seen Betty or Basil? They've been going missing more often lately, and they didn't come home at all last night.'

'No idea, sorry. I'm sure they'll turn up soon!' I called back as I turned onto the footpath and out of sight. As much as those fur-bags annoyed us, we wouldn't force the poor creatures back to that woman – we're not monsters.

I powered down the street, risking a glance at the time – I was so late.

Chapter 2
Is he or isn't he?

I crashed through the back office door, ran my fingers through my hair and took a breath as I dropped my backpack in the corner.

Three minutes late, but it looked like I'd gotten away—

'My wall clock seems to be running hot again, Gabriel,' Murray said, strutting from the kitchenette, '#1 Boss' mug in hand. He sipped his instant coffee – one spoon of coffee, two sugar substitutes, a dash of trim milk. 'I recall we'd agreed you'd give some attention to that, didn't we Gabriel?'

'Yes, we did.'

'Am I going to have to get rid of this… clock? Find myself a new one? One that's more reliable?'

'No, Murray,' I said, gritting my teeth. 'I'll make sure… the clock… keeps better time in the future.'

'Good, that's good to hear. Now, enough chitchat, get to work.' He took a slurp and lowered himself down in front of his computer – a position he wasn't likely to move from for the rest of the day, except to replenish his cup of sludge. 'Our first swingers will be here any minute,' he said, winking.

Every damn time, it made my skin crawl. I get it – the old-timey keys-in-the-bowl type party was the same term as someone hitting a golf ball. Funny the first time? Perhaps – at a stretch. But the twentieth? Not a chance.

Or was he just proud, announcing he was a swinger in both senses of the word? Whether an ill-judged joke or a sad boast, I didn't want to hear it.

To keep our interactions to a minimum, I volunteered to look after the front desk, retrieve balls from the range, tidy up the bays, check on the toilets. Anything that minimised time in the back office.

Once I'd escaped my boss, it turned out to be your standard Sunday, with the usual young families, grandads with their grandkids, and groups of lads. The work wasn't taxing, and I'd been going through the motions all day. Handing out baskets of balls, renting out clubs, and doing an occasional lap calling kids off the grass or de-escalating frustrated amateurs working themselves into a tizz.

Even my lunch – usually a highlight – had roused little enthusiasm. Today I'd made a classic BLT, elevated with some freshly baked bread, sriracha, mayo, and a few slices of avocado. I wasn't one for extravagances, but when it came to sandwiches, no corners were cut, no expense spared. And today I'd inhaled it without even registering.

If Sheela was here, she'd break me out of this little funk.

I looked forward to the shifts we shared. Sheela's in her late fifties and didn't need to work anymore, but she came anyway. On our first shift together she confided in me, saying she'd started working here when her children were young, picking up a few shifts to supplement the family's income. By the time the kids had flown the coop, they didn't need the extra money, but it served as an excuse to get out of the house. 'Get away from my fussy husband, have a few hours to myself,' as she put it.

Lovely though she is, it was a sad state of affairs when this middle-aged mother of three was my best friend in town. I mean, I had close friends back home of course, but I couldn't tell them I was lonely and having a hard time here. I was the one who'd left, after all.

I knew I had to put myself 'out there' as Claire would say, whatever that meant. I attended classes, worked a part-time job, had drinks with people I'd met at uni, made appearances at the gym – all out of the house. But I'd yet to make any real connection with anyone other than Sheela – make an actual friend, let alone a boyfriend.

A boy can dream.

And that was precisely what I was doing as I completed my rounds, approaching the corner of the clubhouse, when a customer charged into me.

He bounced off, arms swinging and about to fall over when I reached out to catch him.

One of the lads – they'd come in a group of three, about my age, and this one in particular had caught my eye. Short brown hair, green eyes, and clearly a guy who looked after himself.

He was a bit of all right.

I'd played a brief, hopeful game of 'Is he or isn't he?' while I checked them in, then thought better of torturing myself.

'Whoa, what's the hurry?' I said, giving him a second to recover before letting him stand on his own.

He stared at me – or through me? – for an uncomfortably long time, as if in a daze.

'You OK?' I said to prompt him.

At the same time another guy shuffled past, heading from the bathrooms back to the bays with one eyebrow raised.

The reaction this elicited from my swift new friend was quite something. His entire body jolted like he'd been shocked, and his face was so expressive, yet indecipherable. Was that guilt? Embarrassment? Terror?

What had happened down there? I considered—

Surely not... Topdrive Golf: gay cruising hotspot? Right under my nose?

No way – I dismissed the thought almost as fast as it came to me. Here with his mates, they'd notice if he'd vanished for a mid-session gobby. This drought of mine had gone on far too long. My mind was conjuring phallic fantasies, and during work hours too. It was getting out of control.

The raised eyebrow, though? Had someone bombed the toilet and reeked the place out?

'I... uh... yes, thanks,' he said. 'Yes, I'm fine.'

Was he feeling guilty at almost being caught out, or just awkward and sheepish about crashing into someone? He seemed to struggle – a lot of thinking going on, but very little speaking. I couldn't decide if it was adorable, or concerning...

'Sorry, I was... I was in a hurry to get back to the tee,' he said with a timid smile. 'My friends will be waiting for me.'

'By all means, don't let me hold you back,' I said, smiling in return and stepping aside to let him past. 'But please try not to bowl over anyone else today. I don't want you hurting yourself.'

'I won't, promise,' he said, frowning a little.

He looked like he was about to say something more, but gave me a tight smile instead, a nod, and headed back to the bays.

What a strange encounter... it had certainly woken me up. My mind was alight – unable to stop thinking about it, turning over what happened. His mad dash, the crash, the varied reactions playing across this face, the stunted conversation...

The result of my preliminary assessment: he was welcome to crash into me any time he liked.

Though not a workable plan, I knew. I doubted I'd manage to contrive working that into a regular part of my day: have inattentive yet attractive guys run into me... I needed another way to get my kicks.

Perhaps I should talk to him? I wouldn't mind getting to know—

No, that's weird.

What reason could I have to strike up a conversation? And what would I say? 'So, you like running fast in inappropriate places?' or 'Nice day to be outside, isn't it?' or 'What did you boys get up to in the bathroom?' or 'You get some good hits in today?' or 'Did you bomb the toilet?'

All non-starters. I had appalling chat.

And even with something decent to say, would I be crowding him if I went over there now? He was alarmed enough from running into me. Though, even ignoring that, it was still strange when staff lingered. Almost like they're trying to join the banter, but everyone knows they're working. An uncomfortable social situation for all.

By the time I'd completed my cursory lap of the driving range, I'd resolved to not be that creepy lurker type and leave them to it.

From the front desk, I overheard bawdy laughter and loud protests coming from one of the bays. What was happening out there? I'd planned to investigate once I'd finished checking in these new arrivals when I caught a short, sharp scream followed by a loud crash.

I leapt from my chair and rushed out, making my apologies as I slid the basket of balls to the latest customers.

Coming around the corner I saw a young family facing away from me, the kids on tiptoes looking over the partition, peering into the bay I'd assigned to the three guys.

There were only two... Where was *my* one?

I closed the distance in seconds to see the other two looking down at their friend – on his back, eyes closed, motionless.

My stomach dropped.

I was in shock, staring, unable to move a step further.

Then one of his friends reached down—

'Don't touch him!' I said. 'Not until we know what's wrong. We don't want to make it worse.'

His friend – the bearded one – snatched his hand back and looked over at me as if scolded by a schoolteacher.

'What happened?' I said as I knelt beside him, dampening down my terror and trying to get control of the situation.

'He swung, then screamed and collapsed,' his other friend said – the clean-cut, gym-toned one. 'Pulled his back, maybe. Is he OK?'

My first aid was rusty... I tried to remember. How did it go? Dr ABC...

D for danger: no, the area's safe. It wasn't a car crash, so no leaking fuel tank or trailing electrical wires or anything like that.

R for response: I clicked my fingers then asked after his name.

'Arthur,' the clean-cut friend said, his voice thick with anxiety.

'Arthur,' I said to his face, then again louder. No response.

OK, next: A for airway. I tilted his head back a little. He hadn't swallowed his tongue – was that what I was looking for? I couldn't remember.

B for breathing: I leaned forwards and put my ear near his mouth and sensed a gentle rhythmic breath. 'He's breathing,' I said.

C for… what was C for? Confusion? Comatose? Chest? Circulation, that's it. 'Is there any blood?' I checked the decking around his head, then touched his hair. No blood, no sign of wetness.

'Do we move him into the recovery position?' I said aloud to myself. 'I can't remember.'

I rested back on my ankles and called emergency services, talking them through the situation. They assured me someone was on the way.

His friends watched on in silence, their clear concern doing nothing to diminish my own. I stayed kneeling, helpless.

The person on the other end of the phone was still talking. They asked after Arthur's status, telling me to do things I'd already done, and reassuring me the paramedics would be there shortly. The calming voice only served to increase my anxiety. Like when you see police officers with guns – apparently there to make you feel safe. But when I see them, I can only wonder and worry why they think armed officers might be needed.

I had worked myself into quite the state of mental anguish when Arthur groaned. I surged forwards, my chest swelling with hope as he cracked open one eyelid, then the other, to reveal his stunning, bright green eyes.

'There he is,' I said, grinning with relief. 'Awake at last.'

Arthur wore a look of confusion and concern.

The bearded friend packed himself in opposite me. 'Thank fuck! Artie-farts, we thought you were a goner.' He smiled too, his relief reflecting my own.

Arthur tried to move as his other friend crowded in too. 'Whoa mate, you stay where you are for a minute,' he said, resting a hand on Arthur's chest.

Arthur being conscious gave me some respite from my earlier despair. But when I'd been considering ways of talking to him again, this wasn't quite what I had in mind.

The paramedics arrived soon after. Murray had checked in, seemed satisfied everything was in hand, then left to go back to whatever he did – useless prick.

I stayed near Arthur's side the whole time. It felt better being there, which might have been selfish of me, but I wasn't going anywhere.

Susan, the paramedic, soon gave us her verdict: strained back, mild concussion. She assured us Arthur would be back to normal in a few days, if he took it easy. Then when Susan raised the need for someone to keep an eye out for him, I saw my opportunity and offered myself. It was a chance to get to know this guy better – wasn't that what I'd wanted only minutes ago when he'd come crashing into my arms? We might develop a friendship. I might make a genuine connection in this town… or maybe more? I was getting some low-key homo vibes from Arthur, even without factoring in what might have happened in the bathroom.

Worth a shot, right? With nothing better to spend my time on, I made the offer.

It sounded like I'd have a few days to test the water, and in his current state it's not like he could run away, I wouldn't even have to tie him up—

No! Don't be dirty. He's injured and I'm not about to prey on some poor, helpless, probably straight guy.

But let's not pretend this was a selfless act. There were obvious benefits for both parties: Arthur would be looked after – most important – and I would have something nice to look at. Perhaps a friendship might develop? Though, I wouldn't mind skipping 'friends' and going straight – for want of a better word – to the good stuff.

Chapter 3
How could I have forgotten?

What was this horror? The last fleeting remnants of my consciousness, desperately holding on to my desiccated husk of a body?

No. No, just a hangover.

After pulling my sluggish brain into some kind of order, I did a mental inventory. My mouth was a desert – standard boozing consequence, easily enough remedied. Then there was the thump in my head – muted yet insistent. On a scale of seven pickaxe-wielding dwarfs dig-dig-digging into my skull, this hangover ranked a solid three dwarfs. I expect Doc, Grumpy and Happy were to blame – bastards, all. The others had – thankfully – taken the morning off… Heigh ho.

With some effort, I propped myself up on my elbows. No surge of queasiness – maybe I wasn't a complete write off today. Things were looking up.

Feeling ready for the next step, I eased my eyelids open and the sun stabbed me in the eyeballs. I wailed, jerking my head back and clamping a hand over my face.

OK, apparently I didn't yet deserve vision. And why was

my room so bright? My flat had many shortcomings, but the blackout curtains were not one of them.

I tried again, my hand shielding the worst of the glare. I started with the ceiling, noticing paint peeling off in a few places, then moved down to see hideous, threadbare curtains – with flowers on them?

My addled brain cells took a full couple of seconds to register what that meant – I wasn't in my own room.

That jolted me awake. I looked down at a duvet that definitely wasn't mine either, then across...

Someone's head rested on the other pillow next to mine, the top of his head a mess of short, brown hair. His chin tucked in to rest on his chest, his arm draped across the duvet, lying on my waist.

I must've moved because he drew his arm back and tilted his head up—

Arthur! How could I have forgotten?

I was in Arthur's bed.

With that piece of the puzzle solved, the week came rushing back to me.

In my campaign to ensnare Arthur, I'd refrained from a full frontal assault – lest I scare him away – but neither was I subtle. I'd laid on the charm, the innuendo and the seduction, skating the fine line between charming and lecherous.

But when we weren't together, my imagination tended to get away from me. Thoughts involving King Arthur doing magical things with that legendary sword of his. It was all very muddled and salacious. Embarrassing too. I would never admit to having such geeky and tragic daydreams.

And I couldn't know if Arthur had similarly lewd

thoughts in private, but during our time together he was a jumble of emotions and reactions. Despite each being plastered across his face, I couldn't make any sense of them. What was he really thinking? Was he amused, shocked, delighted, repulsed, captivated? I had no clue.

I must have struck the right balance though, because here we were.

With my mind all caught up, I looked back at the man in bed beside me. He really was adorable, that face, that chest, and shoulders too – mmm.

The top of the duvet lay across his bare abdomen now… I started to lift the—

No! Don't be such a pervert.

Well… I did see it all last night. And we have been lying together since.

I lifted the duvet to look underneath – oh, yes – I remembered… Excalibur.

I couldn't help but smile as I dropped the cover and looked back up to Arthur's face.

Ew – was he drooling? A thread of saliva hung from his open mouth, and a damp patch spread across the pillow case.

Still cute, though.

I peeled myself out of bed – careful not to disturb the drooling Arthur – and rummaged around for my clothes.

I found my briefs, shirt, and socks, discarded without care in disparate places: on the dresser, in a pile in the corner, on the pile of books by the bedside. Arthur's clothing too was strewn across his vast bedroom. My usual tidy and organised self was not in charge by the time we got back to Arthur's. We had other things on our minds, didn't we?

But where were my jeans? I couldn't see them anywhere and was reluctant to turn things over too much in case I woke Arthur. Had we ditched them before we'd even made it to the bedroom?

I couldn't leave the room only in my shirt, socks, and jocks. Did he have flatmates? I hadn't seen them when I stopped by this week, but they would've been at work, wouldn't they?

I'd have to do the sneak of shame and hope his flatmates – if they existed – were still fast asleep, and not sitting on the couch, coffees in hand, waiting for us to emerge so they could reward us with a round of applause. As unlikely as it sounds, that scenario wasn't the fabrication of my paranoid imagination, it had happened once before. Mortifying.

I slunk from Arthur's room, noticing a door ajar across the short hallway – the bathroom. I dashed in and pulled the door closed behind me.

Oof, I looked tragic. I chugged down a few mouthfuls of cold water from the tap, splashed my face, coaxed my hair into some semblance of order, and helped myself to his mouthwash.

While I gargled, I had a thought – how many toothbrushes were there? Good thinking, Sherlock. Just the one – promising. Or was there another bedroom with ensuite? This could go either way yet…

My head still thumped too, but at least I wasn't in danger of collapsing into a dehydrated pile of dust. And my appearance – not nearly its best, but I didn't scream 'walk of shame' anymore either, nevermind the lack of jeans.

I slipped back into the hallway – it was short, with only Arthur's door and the bathroom coming off it. Next was the living room, dining table, kitchen, and the front door.

No more doors, so it followed there were no more flatmates.

I relaxed, and my hunt for jeans dropped down the list of priorities... Did Arthur have this entire place to himself? Looked like it. But never mind that right now, what I needed most urgently was caffeine.

I scanned the kitchen bench... He didn't have a coffee machine – how did I miss that before? Not even one of those environmental disasters with the single-use capsules. I was getting more and more urgent as I flung open the remaining cupboards – he didn't have a cafetiere either...

Then I remembered, earlier in the week Arthur had said he'd be happy with a cup of instant.

I shuddered.

But what could I do? It's not like I'd head down the street in my current state... I'd have to get by with the instant coffee.

I flicked the kettle on and reached for the cupboard, readying myself for the flood of letters and junk mail. I eased the door open and was pleasantly surprised when nothing burst forth.

Though, I might have preferred that to what I was faced with instead: a value-pack, supermarket-branded jar of granulated coffee. It was just so... big. And the branding... so consistent with every other imaginable item stocked on the supermarket shelves, from dried pasta to butter, nappies to canned cat food.

There it sat, taunting me from Arthur's cupboard shelf, like a mass-produced monstrosity from my nightmares. Patiently waiting, enticing its next victim with the promise of reprieve from caffeine withdrawals. All the while readying itself for an assault on my palate.

I didn't turn my nose up at many things – I was raised better than that – but one does not skimp on tea, coffee, or biscuits.

This was a necessary evil. I needed that caffeine to get to work on the thumping headache, and had to hope I didn't retch from the taste before it got to work.

A generous heap went into each mug. I'd chosen two mugs from Arthur's vast collection. One with a selection of bingo balls and a label promising that 'What Happens at Bingo Stays at Bingo.' The other had a pile of chicken nuggets and the enlightened advice, 'Nugs Not Drugs.' As amused as I was, I still hoped his mug collection was made up of the hand-me-downs or Secret Santa presents he dared not re-gift. He wouldn't have bought these himself, would he?

While grabbing the milk I considered putting together some breakfast. The fridge and pantry were still stacked with ingredients I'd brought over during the week. Enough to make cream cheese bagels, scrambled eggs on toast, or a full English breakfast.

No, I didn't think I could manage any of that in my current, semi-delicate state. Coffee first, then possibly food.

I poured the hot water, smelt that life-giving aroma, took a sip and decided I might survive after all.

It was a short walk back to the bedroom with my two vats of hot, brown muck in one hand, and a big glass of water in the other. I stole a gulp of water before placing the glass and the bingo mug on Arthur's bedside table, shuffling aside some of last night's detritus.

I settled in on the other side of the bed, sitting up to sip my steaming cup of sludge. Arthur had turned in his sleep and didn't appear to be drooling anymore. I watched for a minute before casting my eye around the room. It had been dark last night, and I was preoccupied, so hadn't taken any of it in.

There were, of course, the threadbare window coverings that might as well have been net curtains for all the sunlight they blocked.

A dresser and freestanding wardrobe stood along one wall. Along another he had a bookshelf overloaded with novels stacked haphazardly – some vertical, some in piles – and in no apparent order – not alphabetised or grouped by genre or anything. This was not a curated display designed to impress guests or a backdrop for tasteful social media shots. Simply a place to store his vast book collection, which suggested he might have actually read them. I approved.

Though, much like his mug collection, not one piece of furniture matched another – second-hand pieces, or hand-me-downs?

My picture of Arthur was developing. Everything in this house was functional, at the expense of taste or aesthetics. He either couldn't afford to keep up appearances, or didn't care to. Whatever the reason, the place felt comfortable, lived in. Tidy enough that you didn't get the urge to start picking things up and putting them away, but not so tidy that you felt like you'd walked into a show home.

He was a heavy sleeper, though. I was halfway through my now lukewarm coffee.

I nudged Arthur with my knee. He reacted by snuffling and rolling over, but he remained fast asleep.

I tried something else, something that always worked on dogs – so why not humans? I flicked his ear and sat back up to sip my coffee, nonchalant.

Arthur whipped his head to the side and raised a hand

to rub his face as he opened his eyes. 'Morning,' he said after a moment, a small smile playing across his lips.

'Morning,' I said, returning the smile with the knowledge that I was already doing much better than he would be. 'I got you some water – I know I needed some. And a "coffee".'

'Mm... Thanks,' he said, ignoring the drinks to nuzzle up close to me, throwing an arm across my waist and hooking his leg up on top of mine. He had burrowed his face into my side and was running his foot down my leg when he abruptly howled, flinging himself back and ripping the duvet off. The remainder of my lukewarm coffee splashed over my front as Arthur stood by the bedside, wide-eyed and stark naked.

'You – you're wearing socks. In my bed!' he said, pointing an accusing finger.

'What?'

'No, no. It's fine,' he said, though his face belied his attempt to calm himself. 'It's OK, just gave me a fright... Scratchy, fluffy things on your feet.'

Poor guy, clearly very hungover and trying to recover from his overreaction. I mean, I agreed with the whole 'no socks in bed' policy, but hadn't given it a second thought while I was getting myself together this morning.

'I'll take them off,' I said, deciding to help him out.

'Oh, you don't have to. They're fine, if you want to wear them, that's OK.'

'I've got them off now,' I said, smiling. 'They won't get you.'

His look of embarrassment turned to concern. 'But it looks like I've spilt your coffee... Can't have you in soiled clothes – let me help you out of that,' he said, a cheeky grin appearing.

'Look at you. Way to turn this to your advantage,' I said, more than willing to go along with his thinly veiled ploy.

Last night there had been a real sense of urgency, and compounded by our drunkenness it had been a rather haphazard affair. Fun, though. And despite the banging and crashing, we'd figured it out in the end.

Now, though, it was different. The morning sunlight diffused through the threadbare curtains was almost cinematic. It meant I could see Arthur, head to toe and every part in between. The atmosphere felt relaxed, languid, like we had all the time in the world to enjoy ourselves.

He climbed onto the bed, walking across to me on his knees. He teased my shirt off, dropping it onto the duvet beside us. We locked eyes as my arms came back down, the intensity like nothing I'd experienced before. He came further forwards. I reached out, and he leaned closer, ready to—

Ding dong.

I stopped with my hand only halfway to its intended destination, the spell broken. 'What was that?'

'Mm?' he said, on his hands and knees over me now, too focused on the task at hand to register anything else. He ran his hands—

Ding dong.

He froze – he'd heard it this time. 'Fuck's sake!' He rocked back onto his haunches, thought for a moment, then shook his head. 'Ignore it, they'll go away.' He sounded doubtful – yet optimistic – then, with a smile, he came back to me.

I took his lead – be rude not to, right? I was getting back into it when I heard a familiar shrill from outside.

'Arthur! Are you all right in there, dear?'

Ding dong, ding dong.

'Argh, I'm going to get rid of her,' Arthur said, pushing himself back from me. 'She won't give up otherwise.'

The poor boy looked dejected, defeated – like tearing into your present on Christmas morning, only for your brand new toy to be whipped away by that big cousin you despised.

Arthur pulled on a pair of shorts and grabbed my coffee-stained shirt from the bed. Pulling that on too, he took a couple of deep breaths – steeling himself for the encounter – and left the bedroom.

As I settled in for the wait, I heard Arthur open the front door. 'Morning, Patty.'

'Oh my dear, I heard such a ruckus late last night, and I wanted to make sure you were doing OK this morning.'

'I'm doing fine, thank you, Patty. I'm just—'

'A few drinks last night, was it?'

'Yes, my birthday. I really—'

'Oh, my! Happy birthday, dear boy.'

The inane small talk went on, interspersed with Arthur's many failed attempts to extricate himself.

While this happened, I became increasingly conscious of the press on my bladder – why hadn't I gone before?

They were still talking… Well, Patty was talking…

My need to get across to the bathroom became quite insistent. But the hallway was in full view of the front door. I just knew that gossip-hound would be poking her nose over Arthur's shoulder, hoping to catch a glimpse of anyone he'd brought home.

I refused to give her the satisfaction.

Was there an empty water bottle around here

somewhere? Had to be. I scanned the room – no such luck. My options: the coffee cup, or the window – no, the situation wasn't that dire.

I would have to make a run for it and hope for the best.

My jeans were still missing in action. And Arthur had thrown on my shirt... I could pull on his? Nah. And I didn't want to subject a fresh set of his clothes to my unwashed body either. I could make the dash in my briefs, though that might be dangerous: maximum agility, but minimum defence.

What about wrapped up in the duvet? It would be cumbersome, hindering my speed, but would provide the best protection from Patty copping an eyeful. I decided to go for it.

I pulled the duvet around my shoulders, bunching it up at the front to make sure nothing hung out.

You can't help but feel heroic in a makeshift cape – I could do anything! A quick dart across the hallway? No problem.

And here I go: the covert coverlet caperer, Bedman! OK, as far as superhero names went, it needed work. I'd think about that after I'd finished my toilet break.

The bedroom door creaked as I eased it further open, wincing at the noise. I peeked down the hallway, my view of Patty blocked by Arthur. I had to hope it was the same in reverse.

3... 2... 1... Run!

I started across the small gap, but my foot caught in the duvet before I'd even taken my first step. I crashed to the floor, my head making it into the bathroom, my foot left behind in the bedroom and everything else in between exposed in the hallway.

'Oh! What was that?'

Fuck.

Arthur was soon at my side, looking concerned, 'Gabriel, are you OK?'

Patty was hot on his heels, never one to miss out on the excitement.

I scrambled back up, apologised and reassured Arthur that I was fine – physically, anyway.

I muttered something about needing the bathroom before leaving the duvet behind, taking that final step and closing the door behind me – not before I'd caught Patty appraising my near-naked self.

How embarrassing. I'm glad I'd at least put my briefs back on and didn't burst my bladder in the fall – small mercies.

Overall though, I should have known better, 'No capes!' as Edna Mode would say.

That pee though, incredible. Afterwards, as I perched on the side of the bath – head in hands, wallowing in my shame – there was a soft knock on the door.

'She's gone,' Arthur said.

'Come in,' I said. Let's get this trainwreck over with.

Arthur came in, looking serious. Then burst out laughing, coming over to wrap his arms around my shoulders and plant a kiss on my forehead.

He stood back, looking amused but a little concerned. 'You sure you're OK?'

'Yeah… I just really needed to pee, and she didn't show any signs of letting up. I'm sorry I outed you to your neighbour.'

'That's fine, I couldn't put it off forever. And she was bound to find out anyway. Sooner rather than later, knowing her. At least now maybe she'll drop her campaign to set me up with her niece.'

'A win, then?' I said, hoping that he wasn't just saying these things to stop me feeling so ridiculous.

'A win, indeed,' Arthur said. 'And now that we're up, I could do with a shower. I must reek of booze and bed.'

'And we can't be sure your back is at 100 percent yet, so I'd best supervise, like our paramedic friend Susan advised.'

'That'd be prudent. In case I slip and slide around the place, injure myself again.'

'And I probably stink as bad as you do, so I should shower too,' I said.

'Yeah, you're filthy... But my water bills have been so high lately, we ought to shower together.'

'Save water, save money, save the environment.'

'All right,' Arthur said. 'You've convinced me, Captain Planet.'

'"The power is yours!"' I said, striking a pose.

'I can think of something else that will be mine, in a minute anyway,' he said, tugging at my waistband.

I smiled, and he turned on the hot water.

Chapter 4
Why not double down on the stereotypes?

I don't think we saved any water.

Neither of us were in any hurry, and the scrubbing soon took a sharp turn to the sexual. We got there in the end, though.

'So, breakfast?' I said as we towelled ourselves down. 'There are all those ingredients I haven't used up yet. What are you feeling today?'

'What? No!' Arthur said. 'You've been cooking for me all week. You relax, I'll cook.'

I'd opened my mouth to tell him it was fine, but Arthur shut me up with a kiss.

I almost gagged on the sickly sweetness of the manoeuvre – how embarrassing, this boy had been watching too many movies. But I enjoyed the momentary diversion, so I let it slide. 'All right then, what's on the menu?'

'Uh... Toast?'

I was ready to respond when his smirk cut me off.

'It's the weekend – let's go out for breakfast. Unless you have things you need to do?' he said, looking uncertain.

'Nothing that can't wait,' I said. 'Breakfast out sounds great.'

'Good. My turn. I'll never catch up if I don't start pulling my weight now, Nurse Gabriel.'

'Watch yourself, or I'll leave you on the floor next time you cane yourself.'

Arthur raised his hands in surrender – the towel dropped, distracting me all over again.

'Cheap trick.'

'Worked though, didn't it?'

I laughed. 'It did. Now, put some bloody clothes on, can't be giving Patty another show when we leave the house.'

I retrieved my jeans from the living room floor and pulled them on over yesterday's undies. I wasn't happy about it, but I refused to borrow a pair of Arthur's.

My t-shirt though… Not only did it reek of booze, it now sported a conspicuous coffee stain on the front. Arthur noticed me holding it up – judging whether a rinse in the sink might cut it – and he offered to let me borrow one of his. 'I've got heaps, and they should fit?'

'Yeah, go on then,' I said. It was just a t-shirt, not a ring or anything like that.

He did indeed have heaps, most with some kind of print scrawled across the front. I picked a yellow t-shirt with a small Power Rangers logo on the top left – it fitted a little tighter than I liked, but it would do.

'Mm… Richard was right, wasn't he?' Arthur said.

'About what?'

'Your chest.' Arthur grinned. 'It's nice.'

Already feeling self-conscious, I lifted my hands to cover myself, settling on folding my arms.

Arthur's grin widened as my crossed arms served only to make my chest more prominent. He started chanting, 'Tits. Out. For the boys. Tits out for the boys!'

I pushed him as he laughed, the bed catching him behind the knees and sending him over backwards.

'Is this supposed to be punishment?' he said, still smiling like an idiot. 'You have a nice chest. I mean, I already knew, but that t-shirt shows it off so well.'

'I'm getting another one,' I said, pulling it off over my head.

'No, no, no. Wear it, I like it,' Arthur said, leaping forwards and tugging it back down. I let him.

'This breakfast had better be good.'

'It's my favourite. You'll love it, I'm sure.'

'Let's go, before I change my mind and cook something here instead,' I said. 'And to apologise to Patty for earlier, I'll invite her over to join us.'

'You wouldn't!'

'I would.'

'OK, let's go.'

It wasn't an idle threat. I couldn't allow any more mucking around this morning. My hunger was making itself known, and if I didn't get something in my stomach soon, I'd start getting hangry. And when in that state, I get stroppy. I'm liable to say and do regrettable things, and I couldn't let Arthur see me like that – not yet anyway.

I grabbed a banana on my way out the door to tide me over, just in case.

***

It was only a short walk. And the cafe – it was vast. Set in an old industrial building, double height ceiling with exposed wiring and pipework, light fixtures formed of gigantic hanging whisks. The glass cabinets on the countertop overflowed with treats – both sweet and savoury. There were racks of fresh baked bread behind the staff, with large blackboards detailing the menu and specials in handwritten chalk swinging above. Further back was the bakery itself, with fresh batches of treats being prepared – the scent wafting through was intoxicating. The seating area was one large, open space, partitioned with floor-to-ceiling shelving stacked with pot plants, glass bottles, old-style kitchen scales and the like.

A hipster's wet dream.

And the place was buzzing. The overlapping conversations, customers coming and going, and staff weaving amongst the tables taking orders and delivering food and coffees – admirably not tripping over the small dogs and children scattered about the place – all added to the frenetic atmosphere.

I was glad I'd almost climbed out of my hangover, otherwise this would have all been too much.

We sat at a small – some might say 'intimate' – table near the window. The waitress took our drinks orders – flat white for me, latte for Arthur, and yes, tap water would be fine, thank you.

Our drinks came out quickly, and we put in our food orders right away – I wasn't about to allow our waitress to escape again without getting the kitchen onto my breakfast.

I ordered the Eggs Florentine with smoked salmon and

Arthur ordered the smashed avocado on sourdough. 'We'll never be able to afford a house,' Arthur said, feeling he needed to justify his menu selection, 'so why not double down on the stereotypes?'

'Goodness. We're looking at property together now, are we?'

'What? No!' he said, his face turning beetroot red. 'No, I uh... I meant "we" as in, our generation, not us. Not us specifically.'

'Don't worry, I'm winding you up,' I said. Oops, better not tease too much, can't have him tiptoeing around the conversation.

Arthur went on to tell me more about his friends – specifically Jared and Richard. I'd seen them a few times now, and initial impressions were that they were a pair of louts. But the trio were a tight-knit little crew, one of those rare friendship groups that survived from school, through their further studies and into adulthood. They still saw each other every week, often several times a week. I envied them that. Arthur responded with similar queries, but I deflected them to focus on Claire and Theo instead.

'They sound interesting,' Arthur said.

'That's one word for them,' I said, laughing. 'But no, seriously, they're fine. Our other intermittent flatmates, Betty and Basil, they're all right too. Betty is needy, always eating our food. And Basil can be a right little prick, but he's nice once you get to know him.'

'Intermittent? How often are they there?'

'Oh, most days. The flat can get crowded. Sometimes I wish they'd go home for a bit.'

'Surely you could have a word to your actual flatmates?' Arthur said. 'They'd understand you'd prefer the place to yourselves sometimes. Perhaps set limits, or suggest your flatmates spend the occasional night at Betty or Basil's places instead?'

'What?' I said, very confused. 'Why would they—'

'Well, I presume they're not contributing to the rent... It's reasonable to expect the flat isn't overrun with plus-ones every day.'

'Oh!' I laughed, hard. I struggled to get my breath, and it was Arthur's turn to look confused now, perhaps a little hurt. 'Betty and Basil are the neighbour's cats,' I hurried to explain. 'Not girl-slash-boyfriends. They like to visit us because their owner is a terrorist.'

'Cats?'

'Yeah.'

Arthur laughed at himself then, and I was still chuckling when a different waiter approached our table.

'Good morning, boys,' the waiter said, placing our food down. He was lean and tall, with curly brown hair, fair skin and a dusting of freckles across his nose. 'Arthur, I stole this table from Kate when I spotted you – so nice to see you here again. Though I see you've traded in my other two favourites for someone new.'

He paused expectantly, but Arthur was frozen.

I raised my hand for a small acknowledging wave, 'I'm Gabriel.'

'Gabriel!' the waiter said, delighted. 'Archangel – I'd believe that too. And my King Arthur, what a combo you two make. My name is Noah. Now, I don't own a boat, but if I did, I would gladly have the pair of you on board.' He wore a cheeky smile as he turned to Arthur. 'And who is Gabriel?'

'Gabriel works at the driving range,' Arthur said. He had

found his voice, but still seemed stiff. 'He uh... He helped me when I hurt my back.'

'Oh no, that's terrible—'

'I'm OK now,' Arthur said.

'I am glad to hear that. Was it our Gabriel's heavenly touch that did the trick? And this is the "thank you" brunch, I take it?'

'Uh... Yes.'

'Very good,' Noah said. 'So, what you're saying, Arthur, is I need to injure my back at work so I can have this angel here tend to my hurts? And to show my gratitude, I get to take him out on a little date? Win win.' Noah winked at us both.

Arthur had clammed up again.

'Don't go injuring yourself on my account,' I said with a forced chuckle, trying to make light of the situation. 'I can't go around picking up strays every week.'

'That's a pity, but you know where I am, if you change your mind,' he said to me. Then he turned to Arthur, 'And thank you for bringing your new friend along for brunch, I do enjoy seeing fresh faces, especially ones as handsome as Gabriel's. Now, I will leave you. Please enjoy your food and let me know if you need anything else.' He turned back to me. 'Anything at all.'

'Well, Noah doesn't hold back, does he?' I said once he was out of earshot.

'Uh... No.' That's all I got from Arthur. We ate in near silence for a while, the only interruption to the quiet was a rather awkward conversation that went something like this...

'How's your smashed avo?'

'Good,' Arthur said with his mouth full. Then, after a

brief pause to swallow, 'And your eggs?'

'Yeah, delicious, just how I like them.'

'Good. That's good.'

To say the conversation was strained wouldn't have done it justice. The easy, flirty banter we'd enjoyed before was now a distant memory.

The waiter had made his intentions obvious – was Arthur jealous of the attention directed my way? It's not like Arthur made any attempt to claim me, take ownership, mark his territory or make it clear to Noah that I'm out-of-bounds. So, as far as Noah's concerned, I am fair game. Maybe I am? Though, I had assumed Arthur and I had a bit more going on between us…

Or, perhaps during past visits to the cafe, Arthur had been forced to re-assert his apparent straightness in front of his friends when confronted by this confident and open gay man? For fear Noah's flirty nature might raise Richard and Jared's suspicions about their friend? After years of hiding your sexuality on purpose, I knew the difficulty of the shift. Was Arthur finding changing tack now too jarring? He'd been intending to tell his friends for some time, but maybe he wasn't ready yet for the wider world to know? And felt like he was losing control of a secret he'd held so close for so long?

Was Arthur scared Noah could smell the gay on him – like some kind of homo sniffer dog? Or worried that being seen out alone with me – a guy – people would assume – correctly – that he was gay?

Or did he think he'd come out already and that's all done now? Did he not realise that coming out wasn't a one-and-done kind of deal? I first came out years ago and was still coming out on the weekly. Not that I made a big deal of it, it was just the constant correction of people's assumptions – whether with extended family members at Christmas, casual acquaintances at the pub, or new group project partners at uni. No, I don't have a girlfriend. And no, it's not because I haven't found the right girl.

It's a delicate balancing act of letting them know you're more of a sausages and buns kind of guy, not so much one for the melons and fish taco. But also saying it in such a way as to minimise their discomfort and embarrassment – it's a minefield. But sometimes it's best to just come straight out with it.

You might think it's easier to let someone maintain their erroneous assumption, but sooner or later there would come a time when you'd be forced to correct them. And the longer you left it, the more difficult and awkward it became – I would know.

I almost think it would be easier – more subtle – if I had a boyfriend I could throw under the figurative rainbow bus. It would be simple to respond with the corrected pronoun, 'Yes, I've been seeing someone since whenever. I met *him* at such-and-such a place, *he* is originally from blah-de-blah. Still early days, you know, but *he* is really great.'

Then they'd feel awkward for a second, apologise for their assumption, and the conversation could continue. Everyone's happy.

This all ran through my head during one particularly lengthy silence. But focusing back on Arthur... Were we moving too fast for him? He seemed twitchy, nervous, hyper-conscious. He was here, with one other person – a guy – and it was not platonic. Praise Gaga for that. But was he not ready for this?

It was dawning on me that Arthur's a starter-gay. He

still had his training wheels on, and feared losing control, taking off down the hill and face-planting on the glittery rainbow footpath. Had I stumbled into the role of his gay fairy godmother, in charge of holding his hand and guiding him out into this big, gay world he was only just discovering? It was a lot of responsibility, and I didn't know if I had the energy or the emotional strength to pull it off…

We had finished our food by now, and he'd insisted on paying. We hugged – it was chillier and briefer than I would've liked – and said our farewells. Neither of us committed to our next catch up, instead leaving it open and vague.

I looked at him one last time as we left the cafe and went our separate ways. It might be hard, but if I didn't invest in this guy – wonderful and sweet, adorable and gorgeous Arthur – would I be throwing away an opportunity to make a real connection?

Was he worth it?

Chapter 5
Am I just being dramatic?

'It had been going so well – hadn't it? I wasn't making that up. You would tell me, wouldn't you?' I said, nudging the ball of orange fur.

Basil turned his head, gave me a scathing look and settled back down to sleep.

I'd dropped onto the couch when I got home, daring to pat the cantankerous cat. As if sensing I was in a mood darker than his own, he deigned to accept my proffered pats. Though, on rare occasions such as this, His Royal Highness Basil I of The Couch operated a three-pat-maximum policy. A privilege you must not take for granted. So, despite the magnanimity of this submission, I still dared not go for a fourth pat, lest I lose a hand.

After that, Basil had settled down to sleep through my entire woeful tale, including my thoughts on the aftermath of brunch, of which there were many. Vocalising had helped order things in my mind, even if I hadn't gotten any closer to figuring any of it out.

The only way to resolve my questions or verify my

speculations would be to ask Arthur, but who knew when – or if – that would be?

'Or am I just being dramatic?' I said aloud. Basil still had nothing to contribute to the discussion.

I was being dramatic. I knew it, but that didn't mean I could do anything about it.

And I couldn't just drop this. I hadn't been this stirred up by someone since… I don't know when.

Once I'd reflected on the deflated end to the morning, exhausting myself on my merry-go-round of despair, I thought back to last night. It had been fun watching the easy camaraderie between Arthur and his friends. They'd had a great time stitching him up for his birthday. Then, while soliciting an outsider's opinion on Arthur, they'd given me the perfect opportunity to let him in on how I felt, in a light-hearted and easily deniable way. I followed it up at the bar – when it was just us two – with something a little more earnest. Heart in my throat, I'd made my affections known and my intentions clear – nothing deniable about it.

All it took after that was another round of needling from his mates and Arthur declared to all in the bar, 'Oh for fuck's sake, I'm gay!' The abruptness and the volume of the announcement had shocked me, shocked us all. It only took a second though until I realised what it meant, for him and – potentially – for me.

Sure enough. Wham, bam, thank you Merlin – back to King Arthur's castle we went.

Now, what came next was a surprise – a pleasant one, mind. Arthur may have only been out to his best mates for – what, less than a day? – but he'd obviously been getting practise in with somebody… Or somebodies… No amount of solo exploration or X-rated viewing could develop the kinds of skills he'd put to use last night. He had me fair humming there.

I made a mental note to make some enquiries on that front next time we saw each other… But when would that be?

And here we were again.

Not only was this train of thought frustrating, it was getting boring. Imagine if my train of thought were an actual toy train: the dog would've run off with the extra track pieces so I only had enough to form a basic loop, the toy train destined to repeat five-second laps forever and ever, or at least until the battery died… I admit, the analogy's somewhat contrived, but does it not adequately illustrate my state of mind? I think it does.

OK. I'm bored, you're bored, let's move on…

I decided I should go stare at my course notes for a while. Studying wouldn't set my world on fire either, and I didn't expect any of it to penetrate my brain, but it was more productive than sighing at Basil or staring at the living room ceiling.

My bedroom was the smallest in the flat – the other two occupied by Theo and Claire were palatial in comparison.

The space wasn't really large enough to serve as more than a study or home office, but it fitted a double bed – just – and that's what mattered. The head and one side of the bed were pressed against the walls. On the other side was a narrow channel the width of my body, occupied by the wardrobe and bedside table, leaving a small patch of carpet – the only section of floor in my room you could stand on. And at the foot of the bed was my desk, which hung out over the bed. I studied while sitting on the end of my bed – no desk chair required. An efficient use of very limited space, but it did mean I had to step onto the bed to enter the room. On balance, I was fine with the cramped arrangement because it meant my rent was correspondingly reduced.

I settled in to study, opening my laptop and course notes, then scrolled down my list of playlists. Not one for nature sounds, classical music or other soothing tunes supposedly conducive to learning, I preferred loud and upbeat music. I considered some of my regular mixes – Pumping Power Ballads, Big Beats, Christmas Crackers, and Pride Anthems – before landing on Kick It Old School.

With my study soundtrack sorted, what I needed now were snacks... I pulled my legs up, rolled across the bed and put my feet down out through the door – a manoeuvre I'd now perfected. I got myself a dish of pistachios. They were an extravagance, but... that subtle, salty flavour – chef's kiss.

I settled back down, glancing at my notes while working the nuts from their shells and popping them in my mouth. Unfortunately, this was a two-handed operation, meaning I couldn't make notes at the same time – by hand or on my laptop. And after a few pistachios, I was reluctant to type with my greasy fingers. I needed to wash them before getting back to studying. Might as well grab a glass of water too – the saltiness made me thirsty. I chugged down a glass of water and refilled it to take to my desk. On reflection, pistachios – delicious though they may be – probably not the ideal study snack. And now I needed to use the toilet.

Back at my desk, I checked the time... I'd wasted 20 minutes. But that was enough procrastination, no excuses now, I was ready to get stuck in—

'Gramps!'

'We're hooome!'

The front door slammed behind Claire and Theo as they flung off their shoes and dropped their groceries in the hallway.

'Go away, I'm studying!'

Claire poked her head through my door. 'Uh huh... Looks more like procrastination to me.'

I frowned. She saw right through me, every damned time.

'I'll join you,' she said, jumping up to sit on my bed. 'So, we didn't hear you come home last night...'

'Gramps, out on the lash,' Theo said, grinning as he clambered onto my bed next to Claire.

I should've expected this. I wasn't known to disappear for the night, slinking back the next day wearing someone else's clothes.

'And you've been out shopping this morning, have you?' She knew very well I had not.

'It is rather bright for you,' Theo said, plucking at the shoulder of Arthur's top.

'And quite a snug fit – tighter than you'd usually wear...' Claire said. 'Did you keep the receipt? Or is this a fresh look you're going for?'

I felt judged. I should've changed into something of my own when I got back.

'And what does that say?' Claire said. 'Power Rangers?'

'Power Rangers?' Theo said. 'Hah! More like —'

'Blue! The Blue Power Ranger,' I said, cutting him off. 'That's who I wanted to be when I was little.' Not true – I barely remembered the show – but it was the first thing that came to mind. I would not be discussing my preferences in the bedroom, not this morning and not with these two.

'If Blue was your favourite, why'd you buy the yellow

top?' Claire said. Her mock-innocence was infuriating. 'Wasn't Yellow one of the girls?'

'Well... He does look quite busty in that shirt,' Theo said, cupping his chest.

'It's not mine, OK?' I said. I knew I was spoiling their fun, but I wasn't in the mood for these games.

'Oh?' Claire said, quirking up an eyebrow like she didn't know exactly what was going on.

'You sly old dog,' Theo said. 'Is this the Archer guy you've been running around after all week?'

'His name's Arthur,' I said.

'So... Archer last weekend, Arthur this weekend,' Theo said. 'I didn't pick you for such a scoundrel. Quite confusing with such similar names though, that's dangerous. Could get awkward if you said the wrong name when you're, you know, in the middle of it. Good for you, remembering his name, though.' He nodded his approval.

'What? No, it's just the one: Arthur,' I said.

'Right.' Theo winked. 'Don't worry, player, we won't let your Number One know about this other guy.'

'There is no Archer!' I said.

'Mm... The lady doth protest too m—'

'Oh, jog on.'

'Theo,' Claire said, raising a hand to interrupt any further retorts. 'You misheard. It was Arthur last weekend, Arthur this weekend, and Arthur all the days in between.'

'Thank you, Claire,' I said.

'I mean, how could I forget,' she said. 'You won't shut up about him.'

'I haven't been—'

'And now he's gone and given you the shirt off his back,' Claire swooned. 'Your knight in shining armour.'

'Did he rip your other one off in a fit of passion?' Theo said.

'That's hot,' Claire said.

'No! No, just a coffee stain.' These two lived for the drama and excitement, something I didn't typically provide. They were loving this.

'So when will you be returning the top?' Claire said. 'It's the perfect reason for another rendezvous. Low key, practical excuse.'

'I... I don't know,' I said.

'Perhaps you should take a spare top too?' Theo said. 'You know, for the next time you get a "coffee stain" at his place. And a toothbrush, too. Not that we're trying to get rid of you, but you know, gotta keep that breath fresh. Shows you mean business too.'

'Shh, Theo, that's terrible advice. Gabriel, why don't you know?' Claire said. 'What happened?'

'Arthur...' I said, sighing. 'He's a starter-gay.'

Claire gasped. 'Oh no, I'm so sorry, Gabriel.'

'What? What does that mean?' Theo said.

'What it means,' she said, 'is that Gabriel has a lot of hard emotional work ahead of him, and he doesn't know if he's up for it.'

I nodded.

'Do you...' Claire said. 'Do you think he might be worth it?'

I paused, then nodded and shrugged at the same time.

Claire gave me a small smile. 'Theo, I think Gabriel needs to come to the barbeque with us this evening, have a casual drink and get out of his head for a few hours.'

'Barbeque?' Theo looked confused.

'Yes, the barbeque at Mia's, remember?' Claire said,

quite insistent.

'Oh... Yes! The barbeque,' Theo said. 'Gramps, it's just what you need. Chill out, have some time away from your big gay melodrama.'

My automatic response would be to deny the offer. Claire had gathered an eclectic range of friends – all ages, all backgrounds – and would casually invite me to join her when she headed out sometimes. I appreciated the thought, even if her idea of a good time was often not my cup of tea. A barbeque sounded ideal, though. 'Sure,' I said.

'Perfect, we'll leave you to study and grab you later,' she said as they clambered off my bed. 'Maybe change your top though.'

Then as they stepped through the door, I heard Theo whisper to Claire, 'I hope this Archer guy isn't at the barbeque. That could get uncomfortable.'

'Shut up, Theo.'

Chapter 6
Why'd you let me bring all this meat?

It wasn't a barbeque.

We weren't even in sight of the house and I could already feel the thump of the bass. I looked at Claire and Theo on either side of me as we walked up to the front door. They hadn't dressed for a relaxed, casual barbeque at a friend's place – how had I not realised this before? Claire had done her hair up in one of her going-out styles, not her everyday look. And Theo was wearing a clean shirt. If nothing else, that should've set off alarm bells.

'Where have you brought me?' I said, stopping in the middle of the footpath.

Claire looked almost sheepish. 'Just a quiet, relaxed summer afternoon—'

'—house party birthday rave,' Theo finished with glee. 'Our girl Mia, she loves a rager, and she's got the cash to back it up. Big sounds, trippy lights, hard liquor – it's gonna be next level, you'll love it.'

'Are you kidding me?' I said, incredulous. 'You promised a chill backyard barbeque... and you bring me to a fucking rave?'

'Just a small rave. Gramps, trust us. What you need is a blowout,' Theo said, looking earnest as he put his arm around my shoulders to push me along. 'You're all aflutter over this boy. And as your caring, thoughtful flatmates, it is our honour – nay, our duty! – to get you well and truly trolleyed tonight.'

'Come on, Gabriel,' Claire said. 'What else were you going to do this evening?'

'Well—'

'Stare at your course notes?' Claire said. 'While running Arthur scenarios through your head on repeat?'

I felt seen. She was right, that's exactly what I would've done.

I sighed and looked up as we approached the house. Music blaring, the party was in full swing with people spilling out onto the street, bringing with them the stale smell of cigarettes and spilt liquor.

'Hang on...' I said, lifting the bags of groceries in each hand. 'Why'd you let me bring all this meat? Salads, bread, snacks!'

'We tried to tell you to leave them at home,' Claire said.

'You can't show up to a barbeque empty-handed!'

'It's not a barbeque though, is it Gabriel?' Theo said, speaking like I was a bit slow.

'And how was I to know that?'

'Would you have come if you knew the truth?' Claire said.

'Obviously not.'

'Precisely,' Claire said. 'But you're here now, so you

might as well come in with us.'

I suppose I was already out of the flat... But I couldn't let them get away with this deception...

'Come on you big wuss,' needled Theo.

'Fine, one drink,' I said. At the least it would distract me for half an hour, then I could leave at my leisure.

'Yes!' Theo said.

'That's our boy,' Claire said, squeezing his shoulder. 'You'll feel better for it.'

***

Coming through the front door – stone cold sober – I felt every bit the mature student. Though presumably everyone was from the university, or friends of students, so at least 18 years old. Once I'd spotted a bunch in their mid to late twenties, and a few in their thirties and forties, I began to relax, not feeling so out of place.

There was even someone I knew – we'd gone on a couple of dates earlier in the year. A good-looking guy, and we'd had fun, but he was dull as shit. What was his name? Logan? I think so. As much as I'd tried to get things rolling, after Logan's unending parade of one-word responses the conversations inevitably ground to a halt. Our messaging became sporadic too, we took turns coming up with reasons we couldn't catch up or cancelling last minute. In the end we just ghosted each other – a mutually unsatisfactory end to an uninspiring coupling.

Logan caught me looking in his direction, blanked for a second before remembering who I was, then smiled. It was a sly smile, like a promise of plans for later this evening.

I admit, some of our time had been fun – mainly the

parts not involving conversation – but there was no spark and I hadn't been captivated like I was with Arthur—

There I went, two minutes in and thinking about him again. I needed a drink…

***

I don't know how long we'd been there, but the sun had gone down. I'd had more than a few drinks and met a bunch of Claire's friends, friends of friends, and friends of friends of friends. She knew everyone, it seemed.

There were a lot of people there, dancing and drinking, chatting and smoking. Despite my best efforts, I'd been swept up by the chaos and was surprised to find myself having a good time.

I'd been coerced into playing a round of beer pong, surrounded by a very vocal and invested audience. Theo partnered with me to face off against Claire and some guy – Bennett? Brett? Blake? I knew it started with B. Whatever, let's call him B-Man. You could feel the arrogance radiating from him in waves – he was hot shit, and he knew it. Claire seemed to think so too and had taken little convincing to join the game.

Now, the problem with beer pong, the reason we'd never played in our flat, besides the fact that it's a stupid drinking game – and there's some pretty stiff competition on that front – was that Claire hated beer. B-Man wouldn't let something so trivial impede showing off his athletic prowess, so he gallantly offered to drink Claire's share. And the way he acted around her made it quite clear he wanted to do more than just that. But the offer was overruled when Theo piped up with an idea so ill-advised the mob couldn't resist. And the mob would not be denied. Theo's idea: swap out the beer for shots of tequila. The stuff of poor decisions and nightmare hangovers – the cups were filled with generous portions of it.

I mean, I'm not huge on beer, but tequila? Kill me.

The plastic cups were set out like bowling pins in a triangular formation, with ten at each end of the flimsy trestle table.

'We'll let you boys start,' B-Man said, winking at us. 'Give you a sporting chance.' He draped his arm across Claire's shoulders and squeezed her to his side.

'The condescending prick is showing off,' Theo said, but only loud enough that I could hear.

'Let's wipe that smirk off his face, shall we?' I said, trying to keep it light.

'Yes. Let's do this.' Theo nodded, looking sincere. 'You go first.'

'What?' I said, knowing full well how poor my hand-eye coordination was.

'Show him how it's done, Gramps,' Theo said with a curt nod. He stared down the cups at the far end of the table, as if the intensity of his gaze could influence my shot's trajectory.

Why not go first? It's turn about, so I'd be making a fool of myself soon enough anyway. With little hope of success, I lobbed my first ping pong ball at Claire and B-Man's cups.

It went in!

My eyes bugged out and hands came up in victory, appealing to Theo to join in my excitement. His only response was another curt nod and a look of grim satisfaction, like this outcome was as he'd planned, as it should be.

I wanted to laugh at his earnestness, so out of character. Instead, I tempered my mood – this was serious business for Theo. I hadn't seen his competitive side before. I'll bet in his mind the prize was Claire – quite the motivator, that.

B-Man plucked the ball from the cup, downed its contents, and threw it aside. 'Good start, boys. Only nine more to go.'

The reward for our success? A smaller target for the next round.

B-Man made a show of rolling his shoulders and stretching his throwing arm, holding the ball up for Claire's kiss. She obliged, and he smiled. This guy was a real show-pony, and our growing crowd was lapping it up.

He lined himself up and made the shot. Sure enough, it went in.

Theo snatched the offending cup, knocked it back and crumpled it. B-Man taunted us with a wink. 'One for one.'

'Yes, yes,' Theo said under his breath. 'We can bloody count.'

And so the game went, with taunts and backhanded compliments traded back and forth, onlookers hanging on every word and every move. I tried my best but scored far fewer than I missed. Theo had more success, but neither of us could touch B-Man or Claire who sunk shot after shot, barely a miss between them.

Theo and I were one cup away from defeat. Our aim – which had not been stellar to start with – had gotten progressively worse as we downed cup after cup of the vile liquid. Meanwhile, Claire and B-Man were sitting pretty with six cups still standing.

Theo became increasingly agitated, with each cup we lost making him even more determined to claw back the win. I'd just missed another shot, resulting in a frustrated growl from Theo. I'd never seen him so serious.

Now it was B-Man's turn. Our onlookers leaned forward in anticipation, yowling with excitement and occasionally jostling the table. It would be Theo's turn to drink if B-Man sunk this final one.

He had one arm around Claire's waist as he made a show of preparing himself. Eyes squinted, his other arm held up with ping pong ball poised between thumb and forefinger, B-Man made his shot. He'd gone for the lob and it looked on target. The audience gasped as the ball hit the rim of the cup – the suspense! – then cheered as it plopped into the liquid.

Claire was ecstatic, in that overenthusiastic way that's only achieved with booze and victory. She was bouncing up and down, then hugging B-Man who hugged back and lifted her clear off the ground. The audience whooped and clapped and sloshed drink out of their own cups in celebration.

I turned to commiserate with Theo who'd knocked back the final tequila. Usually so amiable and not at all the competitive type, I saw a cloud pass over his features. He was watching B-Man take Claire for a victory lap on his shoulders.

Since Claire had pointed out Theo's unrequited infatuation, I couldn't fathom how I'd missed it – the love hearts practically bugged out of his puppy dog eyes at the sight of her. Theo was head over heels for her, and this parade would do nothing to boost his self-esteem. In all aspects of her life Claire was so perceptive... But in this, she was the blinded one, getting carried away – quite literally – by this guy. Or was she doing this on purpose? A little show to disabuse Theo of any notions about them becoming an item? If so, it was working, but was also uncharacteristically cruel.

Seeing Theo as anything less than his typical easy, breezy, oblivious self made me a little sad and I couldn't help feeling protective of him. I put my arm around his shoulder, steering him away from the beer pong table and B-Man's macho peacocking.

Theo's scowl deepened as I led him outside into the cool air. The music was still loud, but not deafening, and we weren't hemmed in on all sides by sweaty teenagers or early twenty-somethings. The fresh air cleared my head – I hadn't realised how much I'd been swept up by the antics inside.

We sat on the edge of a raised flower bed, next to a Smurfette garden gnome, and Theo took a swig from the bottle of tequila he'd brought out with him.

'Whoa, buddy,' I said, confiscating the bottle and setting it behind a shrub, out of sight and out of reach. 'That's not lemonade.'

'Such a cock!' Theo said with real venom.

'Hey.'

'Not you. Him,' Theo said, thrusting his chin towards the house.

'He was a bit much,' I said.

'Swinging his dick around like he owned the place.'

I couldn't argue with that. B-Man knew he was all that and didn't mind everyone else knowing too.

'Couldn't keep his bloody hands off her,' Theo said, looking fiercer than I'd ever seen him. 'And Claire's too nice to tell him to stop…' Despite his obvious liquor-fuelled rage, he looked on the verge of tears.

I didn't have the heart to tell him the attraction appeared

mutual, with Claire's hands equally determined to explore her co-winner's form.

'I'm going to confront him,' Theo said, eyes resolute, nostrils flared.

'No, I don't think that's your best idea,' I said, applying some pressure with my arm on his shoulder as he tried to stand.

'Tell him to keep his filthy, grabby hands to himself...'

'That's very chivalrous of you, Theo,' I said. 'But Claire won't thank you for it.'

'And then I'll tell her how I feel,' he said, nodding in agitation, not listening to a word I said.

'Mate, that's another terrible idea. Let's just chill out here for a bit.'

'What am I doing out here?'

'You're chilling with me, remember?' I said, offering him back the bottle of tequila as a distraction – the lesser evil?

He took a swig. 'You're right, I need to get back in there...'

'That's not what I said!'

'Claire won't be able to get away from him – she's too good, too nice to tell him to piss off,' Theo said, oblivious to the irony. 'I need to head him off!'

'Claire is very capable,' I said slowly, trying to calm the situation. 'She doesn't need saving.'

'Yes, that's it! I've got to save her,' he said, eyes alight with devotion.

Fuck, bad word choice. The little dweeb had gone full fairytale on me, picturing himself as the knight in shining armour rescuing his damsel in distress.

'I'm going to save her,' he said again, launching to his feet before I could stop him.

Standing bolt upright, Theo blinked once as the fresh air and swift movement hit him. He jerked his head back in surprise, rocked onto his heels, and stumbled half a step backwards before the edge of the raised garden caught him behind the knees, sending him sprawling into the shrubs.

I'd been transfixed, watching the whole thing as if from afar, not even thinking to catch him. I wasn't as clear-headed as I'd thought... Luckily for Theo it was a plush, vegetated landing and both he and Smurfette had survived the fall. The shrub, not so much.

He groaned as he tried to sit up. Theo didn't have much fat on him, and the tequila had hit big time.

'Oof, I'm... Y'know, drink... I'm gonna – have words. Later. Gonna have li'l nap first,' he said, crashing back down into the bush.

His head was skewed at an awkward angle, mouth wide open, snoring loud enough to be heard over the music.

What was I going to do about him?

I was still staring at Theo, wondering what to do next as a couple brushed past, kissing and giggling on their way to the back of the garden. 'Looks like they're having better luck than you, my boy,' I said to my flatmate's unconscious form. 'I think it's time for us to call it a night, Theo.'

I pulled his legs up into the garden and rolled him over into the recovery position – just in case. That's my first aid training coming in useful, again. This second round reminded me of the first... And I'd been doing so well, not thinking about Arthur, at least for a little while. Claire and Theo were right, this so-called 'barbeque' had gotten me out of my head for a bit. But I wouldn't let myself think about Arthur right now. I had this liability of a flatmate to sort out first...

'Theo, mate, I'll be back in a minute,' I said, even though he wasn't hearing a word. 'Just going to let Claire know we're off, then I'll be back to grab you.'

No response.

'All right,' I said, patting him on the foot. I stood up, a little more slowly than Theo, to be sure the booze didn't rush to my head all at once. If I was the acting responsible adult here, I couldn't be swooning into the garden too.

I squeezed my way through the groups outside, with the occasional brief nod or wave to those I'd met earlier in the night, and had just stepped into the kitchen when I felt two hands grabbing my hips from behind. I stumbled forwards with the sudden jerk of the movement. The grip was firm and rather physical.

I turned, expecting some random who'd latched on to keep themselves upright as they'd stumbled. I didn't expect to be faced with someone I already knew.

Chapter 7
Was it the booze, or the lust?

'Hey... you,' Logan said, like he was surprised to find his hands on my hips, indecently close to my goods. Hang on, he couldn't remember my name, could he?

'Oh, hi Logan.' To be fair, though, I'd forgotten he was here.

'Yeah, so I've been looking for you.' Here we go.

'You have?' Why did I ask that? Don't encourage him. 'I was just—'

'Yeah, you're hot,' he said, bringing his face up close to mine, hands still on my waist – partly for the contact, but also, I suspected, for the support. I'd forgotten how good looking this guy was. 'We had fun. Why did we stop?'

'We both got busy with uni and work, you know.' He didn't need the truth. No one reacts well to being told they're boring – so, so boring – especially when they're half cut.

'Yeah, pity,' he said. 'Well, we're not busy with uni or work right now, are we?' He attempted a sultry look now, and it was only partially successful – the hooded, glazed eyes detracted from the appeal somewhat.

He had me there. 'Mm. But I'm just heading off, sorry.'

'Yeah?' His eyes lit up at that. 'You need some company? I can make sure you get home OK.'

Good try, but not a chance. But… why not? He knows what he wants, and he's got his hands all over another guy in the middle of a party, so he's clearly comfortable being out.

Unlike Arthur.

It would be simple, perhaps we could have some fun, again? It would require little work on my part. Emotionally detached… easy.

But that's the thing. Dating Arthur might involve a lot of work and emotional investment, and it wouldn't be straightforward. But there's the chance the reward would be so much greater. I couldn't let that go, not without giving it a try. Why had I spent all this time flip-flopping in my head? Of course it would be worth it. He would be worth it. And if he wasn't? Well, at least I'd know. I wouldn't be left wondering.

I focused back on Logan. He was smiling, like he'd already won me over.

'No, that's OK, I'll be fine. Thanks for the offer, though,' I said, rebuffing both the spoken and unspoken suggestions. 'I'm letting someone know I'm off, then taking our friend home.'

'Yeah? Is this the "friend" you were playing beer pong with? I was watching,' he said, raising one of his hands from my waist to squeeze my arm.

'Yes, he's had a bit much. We—'

'I wanted to challenge you, but you vanished.'

'My friend wasn't feeling well, so I took him outside for

a bit.'

'He's cute. Is he your boyfriend? We could both join him outside, head further down the garden for some privacy?'

I had to hand it to him, he adapted well to any diversion I threw his way. He was persistent but playful. Why hadn't his chat been this quick before? Was it the booze, or the lust? He might have staved off the boredom, kept my interest for longer.

'Oh, here he is now,' Logan said, looking beyond me.

'Who?' I said, turning to see and catching sight of Theo stumbling towards the house with a look of determination.

'Oh, no,' I said. 'I've got to go, now.'

Logan turned me to face him again. 'We can give your boyfriend a little teaser, entice him over? Or does he prefer to watch?'

Without warning, he mashed his mouth against my own and I couldn't break away. 'No! Get off,' I said against his lips, struggling to get free. But he had a vice-like grip on me, one arm around my waist, the other behind my head, only taking the movement of my lips and body as encouragement. He'd stormed past playful persistence and was now charting towards assault.

'Get off,' I said again, trying to shift my weight away from him and his face, but still he didn't relent. I got my arms up between us, hands on his chest and pushed, and only then did I make any space between us. I pushed harder, straightening my arms and he stumbled back, crashing into another group who screamed in surprise, spilling their drinks as they collapsed into a heap.

I was furious, panting with the effort and the shock.

All eyes were on us as Logan and those around him got back to their feet.

'Didn't have to be such a dick about it,' Logan said, straightening his shirt and wiping his mouth with the back of his hand. He was on his way back to the kitchen – another drink, surely not? – when Theo lurched past.

My flatmate wailed at the top of his voice as he came into the house, 'Claire!' Then again down the hallway and again across the living room, 'Claire! Claire!'

The spectators, having just witnessed our big gay bust up, were now mesmerised by this next dramatic development – some bedraggled shrub-beast coming through the back door and going berserk.

I rushed over to Theo as he climbed onto a chair to shout again. 'I've got something I want to say.'

I'd almost made it through the crowd when I saw Claire burst from the hallway. She looked concerned – as you would with someone belting out your name on repeat. Someone cut the music, resulting in an eruption of outrage. Though this was soon replaced by quiet curiosity as everyone witnessed Theo clambering onto the flimsy beer pong table, scattering the cups of the game still in progress. The players protested, but Theo cut them short by yelling Claire's name again.

He spotted her and a manic grin appeared on his face. 'There you are,' he said, not having to shout anymore with all conversation hushed, expectant eyes swivelled to the latest unfolding scene. 'Everyone, this is Claire. We share a flat, so we see each other every morning and every evening, and even that's not enough. She is the most wonderful, gorgeous person.'

There were a few scattered claps and cheers as Theo slurred his way through his speech, which were quickly shushed by others nearby who didn't want to miss a word.

I'd given up trying to coax him down – he only had eyes and ears for Claire. It looked like we'd be suffering through this disaster to its conclusion. The crowd were invested, they'd even cleared a makeshift aisle between Theo on the trestle table and Claire in the hallway door frame. All the better to witness the romantic wreckage. I checked along the clear line of sight. It was as expected: Claire looked horrified.

'I've never expressed my feelings before, but our other flatmate inspired me,' Theo said.

What was he on about?

'He's older than us, but even with all those extra *years* of experience, he had to learn to put himself out there…'

Rude little shit.

'And it sounded pretty bloody awkward, but he's landed himself the boy of his dreams… He just hasn't realised it yet.'

No comment.

'And the girl of my dreams, well, she's right in front of me. And if I don't say something, Butthead Brad will probably sweep her off her feet for another impromptu parade on those big, manly shoulders of his.'

I knew his name started with B! Brad suited him, I think. That was probably his full legal name too – not Bradley, just Brad. Because that was more cool. And yes, shoulders – even the straight boy had noticed.

'If I don't speak now, I'll always wonder what might have been.'

You could feel the anticipation building, everyone at the party holding their breath, waiting for it.

'Claire,' Theo said, taking a step towards her. 'I—'

And that's when the rickety trestle table gave way.

The legs at one end folded under the weight – not that Theo was a heavy guy, quite the opposite, but those tables weren't designed to hold up anything more than the offerings at your school bake sale fundraiser. One end of the table top slammed to the ground, throwing Theo crashing to the floor, and the remaining cups of beer catapulting through the air. If it wasn't so terrifying, it would've almost been comical – seeing those across from me startled by the sudden shift, splashed by droplets of airborne beer. Though, the main flow stayed the course to douse the now whimpering Theo.

I rushed to my flatmate's side as the house erupted around us – gasps and cheers, ear-splitting screams and bouts of startled laughter. The music was back on, and all but those nearest Theo had gone back to whatever they were doing – the show was over. Claire was there too, looking even more concerned, though for a different reason this time.

Theo was still groaning in a heap on the floor.

'Are you OK, Theo?' Claire said. She tried to lift his head, but he twisted away.

'It hurts,' he said as he tried to sit up.

'Take it easy. Now, what hurts?' I said, giving him the once over. That was when I noticed his left leg – his shin bone, pressed against the skin halfway down – definitely broken. 'How about we lie you down for a minute, OK?'

Despite his state he still heard the strain in my voice and pushed harder to sit up. He had his back against the wall now and looked down towards his shoes.

'Oh—'

That was all he said before he dry retched once, again, then threw up over himself. It was all liquid – all down his front, on his shorts, his shoes and even splashed on his broken leg.

'Oh, mate. It's OK, but try not to look.' I said, before turning to Claire. 'I don't think we can get him to the A&E in a taxi, not with the sick...'

'I'll call for the paramedics,' Claire said, but seemed unwilling to leave his side.

'Don't worry,' I said. 'I'll stay here with him.'

Claire nodded, still reluctant, but headed out the front, somewhere a little quieter to make the call.

I looked back at Theo who had visibly relaxed with Claire out of the room.

'I fucked that up,' he said. 'Big time.'

'Hey, you had to give it a shot. Like you said, no point wondering what might have been.'

'Got to be in it to win it,' Theo said, attempting a smile. 'Though I expect my chances are slimmer than the lottery.'

'The best things aren't always easy.'

Theo looked at me. 'Does that mean you'll give it a proper go with Arthur, then?'

So *now* he decides to impress us with his insights. Though, it is easier from the outside looking in.

'I think it does, Theo,' I said. 'I think it does.'

Chapter 8
Do I get a moon boot?

My perilously romantic flatmate had gotten a few glasses of water down, and after the initial shock of seeing his jutting bone, hadn't thrown up again. I kept busy distracting Theo with inane chat and fending off anyone who came too close – we couldn't have some idiot stumbling by and stepping on his foot. He wasn't groaning so much anymore – was the tequila to thank for that too? It had led us to this sorry situation but was now acting as a makeshift anaesthetic?

The strobe of light coming from the street interrupted my thoughts. 'Here's our ride, mate,' I said.

'I can see the light,' Theo said, wistful, never one to shy away from the melodrama.

'Don't walk towards it.'

'I can't though, can I?' he said, smiling.

'OK, that's enough gallows humour for you, my boy,' I said.

'Goodbye, cruel world,' Theo said, lifting the back of his hand to his forehead.

'Oh, shut it.' I turned and saw the paramedic's silhouette

filling the front door, illuminated from behind by the flashing lights. 'Here comes the cavalry,' I said, getting myself up to my feet to meet them.

And there she was.

'Well, Mr Bedford,' she said over the music, equipment in one hand, the other on her hip. 'Here we are. Again.'

'Um. Hi Susan,' I said, a little sheepish, almost like I'd been sent to the principal's office. She had that stern, matronly way about her, but you took comfort in knowing that despite all that she meant the best for her students – or in this case, patients.

'You do seem to attract trauma, don't you, young man?'

'I, uh—'

'And who is it this week?'

'This is my flatmate, Theo. I think he's broken his leg.'

'Mm, yes. Very astute of you,' Susan said, looking down at the obviously broken limb. 'Now, Mr Bedford, please make yourself useful and clear the room.'

'Right, yes. OK,' I said, but Claire was already on it, shuffling the protesting punters out to the back garden.

'Out! Everyone out, it's a garden party now,' she shouted, then back to me. 'Gramps! Bring the booze and the music outside.' Here's the Claire I knew – the girl with the plan. This was a situation she could take control of, not something so tenuous and often opaque as someone else's feelings.

I nodded, unplugging the stereo to set it up on the patio, speakers directed away from the house. Next I grabbed armfuls of bottles and cups, setting them on the outdoor table, pulling the back door closed behind me.

'That ought to keep them busy for five minutes,' Claire said with a look of satisfaction.

We turned away from the party outside. The house was a mess, with cups and bottles scattered everywhere, the half-collapsed trestle table, jackets and handbags hanging off the back of chairs. But at least it was quiet inside with the doors shut. You could still hear the conversations outside, clamouring to be heard over each other and the music, but they were muted.

Susan and the other paramedic were working around Theo, who clammed up as Claire and I approached.

'OK, we've done all we can here and given him something for the pain,' Susan said. 'Mr Wright, we'll get you to the A&E now. They'll re-set the bone and get your leg in a cast.'

'Do I get a moon boot?' Theo said, looking hopeful.

'No, Mr Wright,' Susan said, patient as ever. 'Moon boots are for ankle and foot injuries. You'll be getting a cast. Fortunately for you, this looks like a clean break, so you should be back on your feet in no time.'

***

'Can we have the sirens on?' Theo said as soon as we got underway.

'No, Mr Wright,' Susan said. 'You're not dying, so we'll take it easy and you'll have to make do with my company for a little while longer.'

Susan and I were in the back of the ambulance, with Theo on the stretcher. I'd offered to join before anyone else said anything. I knew Claire felt responsible and wanted to make sure he was looked after. But her presence would've just set Theo on edge. Though, perhaps he was too calm now – despite the bright lights in the back, Theo was soon dozing.

Susan was busy completing a form, asking Theo the occasional question. After a few minutes, she slotted her clipboard away and turned to face me. 'Now, Mr Bedford,' she said. 'How is my other patient doing?'

I blanked – what could I say about Arthur?

'I trust you've been taking care of Mr Fenwick,' she continued.

'Uh, yes—'

'Has he what,' Theo said, drowsy and slurring with one eye cracked open. 'Gramps here has gone above and beyond.'

'I—'

'Buying the food, then taking the food to his house, then cooking the food at his house. He's a good cook, Gabes is. Don't know if Arthur is though, haven't met him. Just heard about him. I have heard a *lot* about him.' Theo was nodding now, eyes closed again. 'Oh! And Gramps here, he gave ol' King Arthur a massage, helped him in the shower… He's very – he's very hands-on.'

'That's good to hear,' Susan said.

'He's ministered to Arthur's every need,' Theo said. 'And I mean *every* need.'

'All right, shut up now or I'll break your other leg,' I said, growing redder by the second.

Susan quirked an eyebrow but said nothing further. We arrived at the hospital shortly after. I wheeled Theo into the A&E, and Susan handed us over.

'Mr Wright, I will leave you in Mr Bedford's capable hands,' Susan said. 'And Mr Bedford?'

'Yes?'

'As nice as this was, I don't want to see you with another

victim next weekend. Do you understand?'

'Yes, I understand.'

And we waited, just like everybody else.

I'd always assumed the ambulance jumped the queue, straight to the front of the line – not the case. You only got sent right in if you had the Three Fates gathered round, cackling gleefully, with your life-thread pulled taut, scissors in hand. No, most mere mortals were left to languish in the purgatory that was the waiting room.

The bustle of the hospital could be heard in snatches whenever someone passed through the swinging doors – the sounds of other patients being treated. While the rest were left to wait in this miserable space lit by harsh fluorescent lights, and drenched in hospital-grade bleach battling for dominance over the stale smells of booze and vomit and other bodily fluids. Tonight, it was populated by an eclectic bunch of injured drunks, all quietly groaning or dozing, some holding on to their hospital-issued chuck buckets for dear life. A dismal sight not helped by the lone, sad potted plant in each corner. But then, hospitals weren't known for their cheer, were they?

I flicked through the scattering of months-old magazines on the table – titles like Women's Life, The Cyclist's Digest, Home and Travel, Celeb Gossip and Crossword Chat, Fashion and Friends, Motorsport Monthly, and The Practical Caravaner. Did anyone read this rubbish?

The plastic chair bolted to the floor bent as I settled back in to scan the room again. We'd gained another waiting patient, this one with grazes up his arms and across his cheek, but otherwise the room was as I remembered it from two minutes ago.

'Shit.' I fumbled to get my phone out. I'd promised

Claire I'd message when we were here, and to send any other updates. I'd completely forgotten, and we'd already been here at least half an hour.

Yep. Three messages and two missed calls from Claire. I shot back a quick message.

Checked in. Theo is dozing. Just in the waiting room now.

That's when I noticed the message from Arthur. He'd sent it a few hours ago – mustn't have been long after we'd arrived at the party, though I don't think I'd looked at my phone since we'd left the flat. I was busy, OK?

I read the preview lines at the top of my screen.

Hey Gabriel, I'm sorry for being so awkward at the cafe. I hate to make excuses, but I was...

That's it, that's all the preview I got. If I opened it, it would register that I'd seen it. And he'd expect an answer. If I didn't open it, he'd think I hadn't seen it, and he'd be sitting there wondering who didn't check their phone for half a day. I mean, I'm not glued to my phone, but I'm also no Luddite. Who am I kidding? Of course I'm going to open it. I didn't want to play those kinds of games, not with Arthur, and more importantly, I was too curious to read the rest. I opened the message – it was long.

Hey Gabriel, I'm sorry for being so awkward at the cafe. I hate to make excuses, but I was so nervous. I've known I'm gay for a long time, and I do want others to know too, but I've kept it secret for so long that it was harder than I'd thought to have Noah (our waiter) being so flirty. I couldn't stop worrying about people hearing and assuming I'm gay by association, even though it's not a secret anymore and I do want people to know. I'm so glad you were there when I came out to Richard and Jared last night. I had a fun night, and I like you, and I want to keep seeing you, if you want to see me too? I hope I haven't put you off before we've even really started, and I can't promise I won't clam up in future, but I hope you'll give me a shot. Even if I'm still learning how to wave the little rainbow flag. No need to respond right away, but also, please do.

I called it... I fucking called it! The message was tragic, but he was so sweet and earnest about it. The message felt stiff, like he'd agonised over it for hours, then finally committed and jammed the Send button before he could reconsider for the zillionth time. But it didn't really matter what the message said, because I'd already realised I wanted to see the adorable bastard again.

I almost put my phone away, intending to respond later. But considering Arthur had already been waiting hours and had probably bitten his nails clean off by this point, I thought I'd better respond now.

Hey, I know how it is. I felt those feelings once, rode that rollercoaster. I'm gay too, remember? Perhaps you'd forgotten? If you have, I'm insulted. Like a dagger, right in the ego! But also, maybe I can remind you sometime? Not tonight though, I'm a classy boy who won't be summoned for booty calls. That's a lie. But I still can't come over because I'm at the hospital right now.

Better not to dwell on the sappiness via message. We can talk about that in person if he needs. For this message, I needed to lift the mood and get him thinking about what comes next. I hadn't even put my phone back in my pocket when it buzzed – again and again in quick succession.

You're at the hospital?
Are you OK? What hospital?
What's happened?

I realised I could have signed off my message a little better – some more explanation, perhaps? Or simply an 'x' or a winky-kissy emoji? Too late now. I responded again to say I was fine, that Theo's grand romantic gesture had gone awry, resulting in a broken leg, but he was doing OK too – physically, if not emotionally – and I mentioned the hospital we'd checked into. He responded within seconds.

OK, you're a good flatmate. You'll have to tell me all about it some time.

After that brief flurry of excitement, it was straight back to the tedium.

There's only so many times you can look around the room or scroll through your phone. Theo was still snoring away, no good for keeping me entertained. Probably for the best, though.

I'd almost finished counting all the dots on a ceiling tile when I was interrupted by a nurse calling from beside the check-in desk with increasing volume, '—Wright. Mr Wright, please come forward. Theodore. Theodore Wright, please make yourself known—'

'Yes! He's here,' I said after a few seconds. Theodore, of course – I was so used to calling him Theo.

'Very well, and you are?' the nurse said. He looked exhausted, like his spirit had been stomped on and screamed at, and there was no end in sight. But he tried to look friendly.

'I'm his flatmate,' I said. 'Gabriel.'

'Hi Gabriel, I'm Cameron,' he said, lifting a hand to his name badge. 'I'll need you to stay out here, unfortunately,' Cameron said. When I went to object he continued, 'Don't worry, we'll sort him out and have him back to you in no time.' He smiled – it was a nice, reassuring smile – then wheeled the still sleeping Theo away.

'Thanks Cameron,' I said, almost to myself. Poor guy – I felt bad adding to his workload.

I sat for a minute, mind blank, staring at nothing in particular. Then I settled back in my chair to re-start my count when I heard my name belted across the waiting room.

I startled, almost falling off my seat. I righted myself on the wobbly chair and pulled my focus down, the glare of the hospital's fluorescent lights silhouetting someone coming towards me.

Chapter 9
What about Thursday?

'Arthur,' I said, recognising that face right away but taking a moment to reconcile – in my somewhat inebriated mind – that he was here, in the hospital waiting room, right now. 'What – what're you doing here?'

'I uh… I came to keep you company,' he said, looking uncertain. 'I… I know how stressful hospitals can be, but also how boring they are too.' He stood there, awkward, apparently unable to hold his hands still.

'Sit, sit,' I said, patting the plastic chair next to me and sitting up to face him as he lowered himself down.

'How's Theo?'

'What?'

'Theo, how is he?' Arthur said. 'When did he go in?'

Oh yes, Theo, the reason we're here. This gorgeous man had blasted my poorly flatmate from my mind… I wasn't doing well this evening.

'He's just gone in. He'll be fine,' I said, resting my hand on Arthur's knee. It was an automatic, unconscious gesture, meant to reassure, but I saw Arthur tense at my touch and his eyes widen. I whipped my hand back and apologised. How could I have forgotten so soon? I thought nothing of it, it was so natural, but for Arthur – who had only just stumbled from the closet – it was everything.

'Sorry,' I said again, offering a weak smile and folding my arms to keep them to myself. 'I... I forgot.'

'No. No, it's fine,' he said, obviously uncomfortable. Then, he tentatively put *his* hand on *my* knee, 'It's me who should be sorry. Like I said in my message, it might take me a while.'

'I'm in no rush,' I said, looking down at his hand.

Arthur let his hand linger there for a moment longer before taking it back. He looked at it for a second, then up at me, and smiled.

After that uncomfortable little interaction, things relaxed and the conversation flowed.

This whole thing's a bit much, though, isn't it? Arthur turning up unannounced. I mean, I'm quite capable of sitting in a waiting room – those ceiling tile dots weren't going to count themselves.

I had to admit, Arthur was putting in the effort – I might have thought it a touch desperate if I wasn't so pleased to see him. And oh, was I pleased. He was the best thing I'd seen since... well, since I'd seen him this morning. As soppy as that sounds. But my delight didn't change the fact that I was in quite a state – exhausted, no doubt reeking of booze and sporting splashes of Theo's vomit too. If I'd known I'd be seeing Arthur – or that he'd be seeing me, more to the point – I'd have sorted myself out.

This wasn't how I'd pictured our triumphant reunion either. When it came to second dates, hospital waiting rooms were not my go-to... One of these out-of-date magazines was bound to have some sage advice on the matter. I can picture the articles now: 'Six Super Date Destinations to Blow Away Your Beau' or 'Hollywood Hunk Brings Dog On His Date – Woof, Woof,' or maybe 'Bar, Bed and Beyond: Nab Yourself a Man.'

Despite my state and our surroundings, I found I was enjoying myself, and I was glad to have him here.

Though I was conscious of keeping my hands to myself – who knew I was so tactile? I kept going to clap him on the shoulder or the knee, either to punctuate what I was saying, or in response to something he'd said. I mean, look at him – you'd have trouble keeping your hands to yourself too.

It felt like Arthur had only just arrived when an exhausted Theo came clanking back through to the waiting room. Like a deranged spider who'd had a few legs plucked off by some sadistic child, he struggled to operate his new crutches while avoiding putting weight on his casted leg.

Theo was trailed by the long-suffering nurse, Cameron.

'Hey Gramps,' Theo said, barely awake. He hadn't clocked Arthur yet, though his nurse had.

Cameron returned his attention to me. 'He's all patched up and ready to go,' he said, smiling as he handed over papers and pamphlets. 'Here's all the information he'll need' – he looked at Theo again – 'but that'll keep till tomorrow. All he needs to do tonight is keep weight off the leg and get to bed.'

'Thanks Cameron,' I said, putting my hand out to shake. I regretted it almost immediately. It was weird. What are you meant to do here? Unnecessary touching only fuelled the spread of germs, not ideal in the hospital environment. But Cameron humoured me and took my hand.

'No problem,' he said, looking around at the three of us

in turn. 'You boys look after him.' Who was he talking to, or about? A tired smile played on his lips before he turned back to the reception desk.

'What did he think we have going on here?' Arthur said once the nurse was out of earshot.

'I don't know,' I said, laughing, 'but if a little imagination is what it takes to get through a Saturday night shift with the drunks, good on him.'

'I can't even imagine,' Arthur said, laughing, 'dealing with reprobates like you two all night.'

'All right, take it easy,' I said. 'Now, let's get this invalid back to the harem.'

Arthur laughed again – his smile really lit up his face. 'I'll grab us a cab,' he said, heading out of the waiting room. Theo still hadn't noticed him and was practically sleeping upright now.

I fired off a quick message to Claire to say all was well and that we'd be home soon.

'OK, mate,' I said, nudging my flatmate on the shoulder. 'Let's get you home.'

***

'I am so ready for bed,' I said, the movement and the hum of the vehicle lulling me ever closer to sleep.

'Theo looks like he's well overdue,' Arthur said from the seat in front of me.

'That he is,' I said. 'I'm not far off either.'

Hang on, did Arthur expect to come in? Oh no, that would not be happening. I knew my room was tidy – always is – but the rest of the flat was a dump. Theo's half-finished paintings and sculptures, Betty and Basil's hair everywhere, dishes on the bench. Even if the flat was looking fresh, I certainly wasn't. Stuck in that weird limbo where I wasn't sure if I was still drunk, hungover, hungry, or just exhausted – probably a combination of them all. And that's not even considering my unwashed pits and bits...

In summary: no state to be hosting.

We might've been able to get away with it if we were in similar states of disarray, but that was not the case here. Now, I needed to make it clear he wouldn't be coming in, but also that I very much wanted him to, just not tonight. Blaming it on Theo would be a legitimate excuse, but could also be seen as me taking an easy out...

We'd turned onto my street when Arthur spoke up. 'Will you need a hand getting Theo inside?'

There it was. 'No, no. We'll be all right. He's got *some* control over his crutches now,' I said, laughing. 'I'll get him inside, force some water down, chuck him in bed, and I'll be conked out right after.'

'Yeah, you must be—'

'I would offer you a drink or something, but...'

'Oh, no. No, that's OK. You guys must be shattered, I'll head home,' he said, brushing away the non-offer. Then added a little more tentatively, 'Perhaps we could try another day?'

'Yes, that would be – just there, please,' I said to the driver as we approached the flat.

'Right you are, boss,' he said, pulling across the road into a space outside our building.

'I'll help you get him out of the cab at least,' Arthur said, telling the driver he'd be back in a second as he came around the other side of the car.

I jostled Theo awake. 'Mate, we're home, get up.'

All I got in response was an unintelligible mumble as he nestled against the seatbelt and returned to his drunken slumber.

I got out and clomped around as Arthur opened the door. He grabbed Theo's crutches as I hefted my flatmate out of the car. He'd woken up enough to put his arms into the crutches – the cool night air would've helped jolt him awake as the alcohol-blanket faded.

We stood on the footpath by the cab, watching Theo hobble to the front door. The temperature had dropped, and I felt goosebumps on my arms, but wasn't in a rush to go inside – that would mean Arthur had left and I'd be alone again.

'He'll be all right,' I said.

'Yeah,' Arthur said, turning back to me. 'So, this week sometime?'

I smiled at his eagerness. 'I'd love to. How about Tuesday?' Not your typical date night, but I didn't want to wait until next weekend either if I could help it.

'Tuesday's bingo night,' Arthur said, his disappointment obvious, 'and I can't let them down.' He shook his head a fraction, then added hopefully, 'How about Wednesday?'

'Ah! No. I've got my late shift at the driving range. Murray will dock my pay if I change my shift without at least a couple month's notice,' I said, frustrated with how much power that prick had over me. 'What about Thursday?' This was more difficult than I'd thought. Despite our eagerness, we were almost at next weekend again anyway.

'Yes,' Arthur said, his face a mixture of relief and delight. 'Thursday's perfect.'

'Great,' I said, my expression reflecting his. 'Dinner at

mine? I'll cook.' I knew Arthur needed more time – you don't become openly and comfortably gay overnight. We'd continue easing him out into the wider world later. Dinner at home would put on less pressure than out in public. I hoped it would allow him to relax and be more himself. Let's call it a practice date. And there were so many things we could practise together.

'You... you can't do that! You've already done too much—'

'It's OK, I'm happy to cook,' I said. 'Don't worry, I'll give you plenty of opportunity to repay me after dinner.'

Arthur grinned. 'I can do that.'

'I know you can,' I said, smiling back. Then a little more seriously, 'Thank you for coming in tonight. I was glad to have you there.'

There was a moment of silence before Arthur leant in. The movement was almost imperceptible, but I took his subtle cue and leant in too. Our lips touched. Where the cool air had merely nudged me towards wakefulness, the contact with Arthur blasted away any lingering lethargy. He had his arm around my waist, pulling me closer. The full lengths of our bodies pressed against each other as we kissed, caught up in—

Honk honk.

'Boss, you coming or staying?'

We startled apart, Arthur's face bright red.

'Uh, yes,' Arthur said, stuttering to the driver. 'I'm coming.' He shuffled on the spot, too embarrassed now to even make eye contact with me.

How had we forgotten about the driver? He was sitting right there, window open with his elbow resting on the door, fingers strumming the top of the door frame, and a wry smile on his face. The bastard did that on purpose.

'Thursday,' I said, putting my hand on his arm for a second.

'Yes, yes! Thursday,' Arthur said, nodding and looking at our feet.

'I'm looking forward to it.'

At this he looked up and grinned. 'Me too.'

Arthur turned back to the cab. I shot the driver a filthy look, and he smirked in return.

I waved as they pulled out, sighed, then made my way back to the flat, retrieving a dozing Theo from the shrubbery on my way.

Chapter 10
What's for dinner?

Murray had been shaking with impotent rage for the past ten minutes – ever since Sheela's shift was due to start – but said nothing as she bustled into the office. He stayed at his computer, simmering away.

'There he is, my favourite boy in the whole world. Hello sweetie,' Sheela said with a wide grin of delight as she closed the door and dropped her over-sized handbag on the table. Sheela's a woman of Pakistani descent in her late-fifties, wife, mother, part-time driving range employee, and all round good sort. She was also my best friend in town. 'Don't tell my sons I said that – I love them dearly, but they're little bastards sometimes.'

'Hi Sheela,' I said, accepting her big, warm hug and a kiss on the cheek. I'd never met her children, but she spoke of them so often it was as if I knew them already.

'We've got pakora today, sweetheart,' she said, pulling out her airtight container.

'Spicy, deep-fried potato fritters, what's not to love?' These were one of my favourites, and Sheela took them very seriously. They needed to be a perfect golden brown – not yellow, not brown, golden brown. Slightly puffy, but still crispy – not soft or soggy. Packed with potato, onion, chilli, coriander, cumin, and all the rest – delicious. And that sweet, spicy, deep-fried aroma as I lifted the lid – I was drooling in anticipation.

'Absolutely, my dear.' She whipped out a smaller container. 'And a tamarind chutney for dipping.'

I dunked and devoured one – still warm! – followed by another, and another after that. 'These are your best yet, Sheela,' I said around a mouthful. She'd given me the recipe, along with those unwritten tips that make all the difference, but I still couldn't make them like Sheela did.

'Oh, rubbish – you say that every week. You just haven't had any dinner, have you, my boy?'

'I have... but that was at least an hour ago,' I said, still chewing.

'Stop talking with your mouth full,' Sheela said, swatting my hand as I tried to grab a fourth. 'Chew properly or you'll choke.'

'So good though, nice kick too,' I said, giving her a cheeky smile as I dunked my fourth into the chutney. They really were very good. I wasn't only saying that to keep this snack train rolling – they were divine.

'Yoohoo, Mr Manager, would you like some?' Sheela said.

Murray jerked back from his computer monitor. He had been studiously ignoring us, pretending to focus on his spreadsheet. 'Would I like some what?'

'Pakora.'

'Pack-a-what?'

'Pakora.' I knew Sheela – if Murray didn't bother even

attempting to say it properly, she wouldn't bother enlightening him.

A pause from Murray, obviously waiting for something more. And when nothing was forthcoming, deciding he'd rather turn down the offer than expose his ignorance, he said, 'Oh, no. I don't think so. Full from my dinner.' He patted his stomach. 'Debbie made my favourite: sausage, mash, and peas.'

'Very well,' Sheela said, and turning back to me she added under her breath, 'Sausage, mash and peas... What a dreary meal.'

'I mean, there's nothing wrong with it,' I said, 'but I doubt I could rustle up any enthusiasm for a humble sausage, mash, and peas.'

'A sad meal for a sad, sad man,' Sheela said, tutting.

With pursed lips and flared nostrils, it was obvious Murray didn't approve of our little snack and chat sessions. I mentioned this to Sheela once, and she said not to worry, that she'd been working here since before Murray had even cultivated his first wispy moustache, and that though his badge had 'Manager' written on it, everyone understood who was in charge. 'I do enjoy needling our Murray, remind him who really runs the show,' she'd said, winking at me. But unlike Murray's, her wink was akin to a comforting embrace, drawing me into her confidence.

I reached for one more, looking at Sheela out of the corner of my eye – was she going to let me?

'Last one, young man, or you'll go to fat,' she said, slamming the lid back on the container. 'That's enough for tonight, you can take the rest home with you.'

Ding.

'I'll get it,' I said, ducking out to the front reception

before Murray could scold us for leaving it unattended. It was another of our regulars, David – kept to himself mostly, an accountant, Sheela had informed me once. He was here every Wednesday evening at the same time without fail. An hour at the tee – no more, no less – and he was off again.

By the time I'd checked him in, Sheela had settled down in the fold-out chair beside me.

Wednesday was late-night at the driving range. Murray would head home soon, leaving us to run the show. It was always quiet, never more than a trickle of regulars. And they all knew the drill, didn't need any help from us. That left me and Sheela free to gossip to our hearts' content until it was time to lock up the place.

'So then, young man,' Sheela said, 'how did it go? Have you got any updates from Friday night?'

Did I what. I don't think I'd ever stacked up so much content for Sheela in one short week.

I couldn't help myself from smiling. 'It went well.'

'Yes, it looks it,' she said. 'Go on, tell me everything.'

'Well—'

'And don't you glaze over the good bits either,' Sheela said, slapping the table for emphasis. 'I may be knocking on sixty, but that doesn't mean I shy away from all the sordid and salacious details.'

'What a hussy!'

She winked in response. 'Let's hear it.'

I did my best to recount everything, with Sheela interjecting regularly for more details. And I did skim by the X-rated parts despite her insistence. Friday night at the pub for Arthur's birthday, then our two-man after-party back at his place. Saturday morning out for brunch with him, and Theo and Claire's 'barbeque' that afternoon. Our trip to the hospital, and my offer to cook him dinner tomorrow night.

'At your place?' Sheela said.

'Well, yes,' I said. Where else?

'Even though he has a place to himself? With no flatmates?'

'That... that might have been easier...'

'And you've cooked at his place before, so you already know your way around.'

'Sheela, where were you on Saturday night? I needed your wisdom!'

'Don't beat yourself up, sweetheart,' she said, patting my knee. 'You were soaked in tequila and practically sleepwalking by that point. Not at your best, I'm sure. Be glad you had enough wits about you to send him home.'

'Yeah, that could've been a fail,' I said. 'But anyway, maybe next time I'll invite myself to use his place. For tomorrow night, I've already told Theo and Claire they have to be out of the flat. They didn't even argue.'

'Feeling guilty, are they?' Sheela said. 'For dragging you out to the "barbeque"?'

'Probably,' I said, laughing. 'And grateful I was there when it all went to shit, so I could take Theo to the hospital.'

'Imagine if it was Claire in the ambulance with him – the poor kids would've died of awkwardness.'

'They're both still tender after Theo's great proclamation,' I said. 'They can be in the same room as each other now. So, that's a step.'

'OK. So, you've got the place to yourself?'

'Yes.'

'Now,' Sheela said, facing me with a look of such gravity I had never witnessed before. 'What's for dinner?'

'This is the thing – I have a few ideas, wanted to run

them past you. I've cooked them all before, but I'm not sure what to go with.'

'Hit me.' She nodded.

'Roast lamb—'

'How are you cooking it?'

'Slow cooked, five hours. On a trivet of onion, carrot, celery, fresh herbs. And wine.'

'You're using that for the gravy?'

'Yes, I—'

'And veggies to serve?'

'Potatoes – crisp and crunchy on the outside, soft and steamy on the inside. Carrots and pumpkin. Broccoli and cauliflower with cheese sauce.'

'Mint jelly?'

'Mint sauce.'

'Good, good,' she said, nodding. This was serious business, the quick-fire questions like an interrogation. It's what I needed though, someone I could trust to scrutinise the menu, make sure I wasn't forgetting something. 'And what's option two?'

'Firecracker beef brisket.'

'Oh yes, here we go,' Sheela said. 'How are you doing it?'

'Season and sear the beef, then brush with paprika, mustard powder, cinnamon, chilli flakes, golden syrup and all that. Garlic, bay leaves, chillies, onions, and the sauces. Cover with foil, then in the oven on low heat for six hours. Another stir and brush, then turn the oven up for a bit longer until dark and sticky. By then it just falls apart, so juicy, sweet and spicy.'

'Mm mm mmm. Oh yes, I think I'll swing by tomorrow night, make sure it's up to scratch, you know.' Sheela smirked.

'Hah! Not a chance. Don't worry, I'll do a big batch and put some aside for you.'

'That's my boy,' Sheela said. 'And any accompaniments? Or is option two a full-on meat feast?'

'Some coleslaw and bread.'

Sheela nodded. 'Yes, that beef sounds like it'd pack a punch, you'll need something simple to go with it. So… Five hours for the lamb, six for the beef – you don't do things by halves, do you sweetheart?'

'I—'

'You're right though, can't be serving your future husband beans on toast.'

'Future—'

'Don't worry, once you've had him around as long as I've had Iqbal, you can get away with beans on toast,' Sheela said, back to patting me on the knee. I realise I'd said I wanted to give this thing with Arthur a proper go, but I didn't want to be getting ahead of myself. Sheela wasn't coy when it came to sex and dating and all that, but she was still a mother who wanted to see her children – honorary offspring such as myself included – happy and settled, eventually.

'Now, your third option?'

'Chicken—'

'Boring,' Sheela said, cutting me off.

'But—'

'No. Chicken is the missionary position of the meat world.' She tutted, like she was disappointed in me. 'Perfectly serviceable for your average weeknight in front of the TV, but not for a hot date coming over for a hot meal and some hot, sweaty—'

'Whoa. Sheela. Hear me out,' I said. And waited.

'Fine!'

I quirked an eyebrow, waiting for the follow up comment. 'Braised chicken with chorizo and olives.' Still no comment... maybe she would hear me out after all? 'I'll get *layers* of flavour from the different forms of salt. Sea salt the chicken, as usual. Thighs and drumsticks – not sad, dry, flavourless chicken breast. Seared. Brown the onion in the chicken fat. Fennel, rosemary. Then I'll layer on my different salts: briney from the green olives, and meaty and fatty from the chorizo. Garlic, oregano, chilli flakes. Then white wine, cook that down. Tomato paste, cook that down. A little flour to thicken the sauce. Chicken stock, lemon juice, bay leaves. I'll have a liquidy, saucy mixture which will come about halfway up the chicken in the roasting dish. Reduce the sauce down in the oven for an hour and a half, basting every half hour, letting all the flavours meld in the meat. Really tender. Not dry heat like roasting, not wet heat like stewing – the perfect Goldilocks zone. And served with a creamy polenta mash. That soaks up the sauce on your plate too, takes on the—'

'OK, OK. That's enough,' Sheela said, eyes closed, one hand up to stop me, the other on her chest as she took deep breaths. 'That's the one. I'm in love already.'

'What?'

'I take it back, I apologise,' Sheela said, flapping her hand at me dismissively. 'That sounds divine. After eating that, if Arthur doesn't get down on one knee – or two knees for that matter – then he doesn't deserve you.'

'So, those are my options. Thoughts?'

'Right, yes,' Sheela said, having calmed herself she was back in business mode. 'So we've got lamb roast, beef brisket, and not-boring chicken?'

'Yep.'

'The roast. If you do this properly – as I trust you will – you'll have a juicy, tender roast lamb, crunchy potatoes, delicious vegetables, all doused in a thick, hot, tasty gravy. It's a classic. A people-pleaser, it never goes out of fashion.'

'Yes, yes!'

'Like a big, warm hug from grandma.'

'Uh…'

'Cosy and cuddly… Is this the vibe you're going for?'

'Not – not so much.'

'And heavy. Roasts are all about big portions – piling it on your plate, followed by sinking into the couch for a nap while you digest.'

'Yeah… I don't want to put him to sleep.'

'Exactly! You want to be bouncing around on top of each other. A loaded plate of grandma's finest doesn't lend itself to that.'

I was speechless as the colour rose up my neck. Not that I was a prude, but Sheela wasn't holding back tonight.

'I think we put that one aside. Roasts are Sunday dinners for a reason,' Sheela said, elbow on the bench, staring at me now. 'Option two: firecracker beef brisket.'

I nodded. Good, yes, let's move on.

'How much spice can this white boy handle?'

'What?'

'Well, it sounds delicious, but you'll be packing in a lot of spice. If you're heading down there' – she nodded down to my seat – 'you don't want Arthur explod—'

'Right! Yes, no firecracker for the white boy,' I said. If I was feeling a little flushed before, now I was full red.

'Mm, thought so. Might put a dampener on the

evening... You can cook that again some time though, I must try it. Perhaps some time you won't be having your overnight guest?'

'Yes, another time.'

'And then there was one. I think your not-boring chicken will be perfect, Gabriel. Much less of a time commitment than the other two. Substantial enough to sustain you boys for the evening—'

'Sheela!'

'—but not too hefty in the gut like the roast would be. And plenty flavoursome without irritating Arthur's white boy tummy – just make sure you're not too heavy handed on that chilli, hmm?'

'Yeah, I might ease off a little on—'

'He's a lucky boy, that Arthur,' Sheela said, looking at me like a proud mother.

'Hah. Thanks Sheela.'

'And for dessert?'

I grinned – my turn to bring down the tone.

She slapped me on the shoulder and smiled. 'Oh, you scoundrel,' she said. 'It's almost a pity all that effort you put into preparing dinner will be forgotten.'

'I can live with that... And I'm sure it'll be worth it,' I said. What a sap. But I couldn't help it.

Sheela smiled and squeezed my shoulder. 'I'm sure you're right.'

Chapter 11
Let's have a look then, shall we?

I had plenty of time.

Once this tutorial finished, I'd drop by the supermarket to pick up dinner ingredients, and some booze too. That'd give me all afternoon to cook, tidy up the flat, shoo my flatmates out, and wash my bits – it's a date, got to be fresh.

Why did I bother coming to uni this morning? I was taking down the notes, but wasn't taking anything in – leaving the coursework for future-Gabriel to decipher. This is something you can get away with on occasion, as long as you don't leave *everything* up to future-you to process or you'll drown come exam time. Top study tip, all yours, free of charge. And do let me know if it works for you. I haven't managed to pull it off yet myself, but I remain optimistic.

Anyway, I'm at uni – as I should be – because I won't need *all* day to prepare for tonight. Claire and Theo would get under my feet anyway, making new messes to replace any I'd just cleared. Theo was my likeliest culprit – knowing him, he'd decide today's the day his muse had descended from on high to anoint him with the inspiration for his magnum opus. And there would be nothing for it but to create – letting it flow through him and into his masterpiece. It was anyone's guess what form that might take. This week it might be a wall-spanning mural of youth and nature and beauty, next week a life-sized sculpture of his most frequently featured subject, Claire. No matter what, it would involve turning the flat into a bombsite of paint, canvas, plaster, clay, whatever.

And Claire – so good in so many respects, tidy and courteous and an all-round good person to live with – was notorious for leaving dirty coffee mugs strewn about the flat. A small thing, but it irked, and I couldn't have that today.

Kicking them out for the entire day and night was an option, but I didn't want to push my luck. Best to be out myself this morning and let them do... whatever it is they do. Then, mid-afternoon, I'd shuffle them off. They seemed to be getting back to normal too – not scarpering in embarrassment whenever the other entered the room – and Theo was pretty mobile these days, though slower and more clunky than usual with his plastered leg. They'd had all week to prepare themselves, with daily reminders from me. Moral of the story: they had no excuses, and I would not allow them to cramp my date.

Laying this groundwork did little to distract me from the feelings I'd experienced this week while waiting to see Arthur again – the strength of which surprised me. But with his work, my classes, and our misaligned weekday evening schedules... Thursday was it. Perhaps I should've pushed for earlier – Monday night? Or even Sunday – mere hours after seeing each other at the hospital? No, I mustn't appear desperate.

There's still plenty of time – today, and for 'us' in general. It was still hours until I expected a knock on the front door, and we had all the time in the world to get to know each other, if that's what we wanted. I appreciated all this, but still, waiting was frustrating.

I arrived home, dropped the groceries on the kitchen floor and surveyed the flat. Not as bad as I'd feared. There were a few dishes on the bench, Basil curled up on his perch – courteously restricting his shedding to one spot, minimising the zone of ginger hair fallout – and the usual selection of Theo's half-finished works I could shunt over, if not out of sight, then at least confined to the corner.

And then there was Theo himself, looking bleary and dishevelled, wearing only boxer shorts as he stumbled from his room with his arms in crutches and one foot clonking on the floor. The automatic air freshener sensed his movement and sprayed its mist – the flavour of the month: 'Essence of Citrus.' Claire had positioned it atop the cabinet outside Theo's room to activate whenever he entered or exited his den of squalor, masking the stale smell emanating from within. For someone who showered and bathed like water bills were something that only happened to other people, Theo was a filthy creature. His clothes washing system seemed dominated by a sniff test that wouldn't detect anything over his room's ambient stench anyway. And his bedding... I don't think he'd washed it since we moved in, which was months ago. And who knew if he'd even recognise our vacuum cleaner. Hardly the behaviour of someone trying to impress their flatmate. But the inconsistency was very on-brand for Theo.

Had I woken him when I shut the front door?

'Hey, Theo.'

'Morning, Gramps,' he said, then noticed all the groceries and perked up. 'Tonight's the big show, is it?'

'Yes, it is.' As if he wasn't well aware.

'Don't worry, old man,' he said, flapping a hand. 'Just going to have a shower, then I'll start on a quick portrait of you. Full body, life-sized! Something for you to give Arthur – a party favour! – to hang on his wall. Or do you think he'd prefer to receive it from the artist himself?'

'Fuck off, Theo. What are you really doing?'

'Don't you think he'll like it?' The little shit smirked, enjoying seeing me all worked up over this boy.

'He'd love it, I'm sure,' I said, grinding my teeth.

'Chill, Gramps. Claire and I will be out of your hair, as you've asked, and reminded us *ad nauseam*,' Theo said. 'We're doing BYO at the Thai place with some friends, then karaoke.'

Yes, good. That'll keep them out of the house for a good chunk of the night.

'And how will you be entertaining your guest this evening?'

'I'm sure we'll think of something.'

'I'm sure you will.' He made some childish kissing noises, smiled, then clomped the rest of the way to the bathroom.

They'll be gone soon enough. That would be this afternoon's mantra.

I was putting the groceries away when Betty appeared from nowhere to investigate, a lump of white fur rummaging amongst the bags.

'Oi, out of it.' Her only response was to fire up the purr-machine as she continued to forage. 'I'm telling you off here,' I said, lifting Betty from amongst the groceries and putting her down on a bag I'd already emptied. She loves a bag – canvas, jute, plastic, doesn't matter what – and was still purring as she curled up and went to sleep on one of them. If only my flatmates were as easily pleased and well behaved – mostly – as these cats.

With the food put away, I started on dinner. It was still plenty early – hours until Arthur arrived – but I could leave it in the oven on low heat to keep it warm. I was only up to searing the chicken when I heard crashing from the bathroom. I switched the gas off and ran towards the swearing. The door was locked, so I banged on it, calling out to Theo.

'Fine! I'm fine,' he said, his voice muffled by the door and the shower.

'You shouldn't lock the door, Theo,' I shouted through the closed door. 'You know, in case you cane yourself properly in there.'

I heard the water turned off, a clattering of crutches and more swearing, then a slow clomp to the door. Theo unlatched and pulled the door open.

'Happy, mother?' he said, huffing with the effort. He had a towel around his waist but was still sopping wet.

'What happened?'

'I slipped.'

'Yes… how did you slip?'

Theo sighed. 'I was reaching to turn the tap off. But don't worry, I caught myself. Only knocked it a bit,' he said, nodding down at the broken leg he'd waterproofed with a black bin bag.

'Probably shouldn't use crutches on the wet floor either.'

He rolled his eyes and shut the door in my face. He didn't lock it though – good. I returned to the kitchen – he'd scream again if he needed help. I wasn't about to towel him down, he could manage that himself... Supervising invalids in the shower – how had that become my thing?

When I stepped back into the kitchen Betty was on her haunches in front of the stove, coiled up and ready to pounce. 'No!' Betty shot a look at me, up at the stove, back at me, then released the tension she'd built up. Caught in the act, she changed tack and trotted over to me, meowing hopefully. 'Yes, yes, OK.' I dropped a small piece of fatty, raw chicken from the plastic tray onto the floor. Betty snatched it up and settled in near my feet, ready for any more dropped morsels.

I was preparing the sauce as Claire emerged from her room, looking her glamorous, relaxed self. Normally one for trainers, tonight she sported some flashy heels – strictly prohibited on the wooden floors according to our tenancy agreement, but Claire was careful to keep pressure off the heels. Despite this, and the fact they couldn't be comfortable, she made it all appear effortless.

She quizzed me on my plans for the evening while I cooked and Theo finished getting himself ready. 'Sounds like you've got everything planned out,' Claire said, hip resting on the kitchen bench, looking at me with amusement. 'Try to go with the flow though, hey? See where the evening takes you, OK? Be flexible, not too stiff.'

'That's the whole idea, though, isn't it Gramps?' Theo said with a chuckle. 'Later on, anyway.' I hadn't seen – or heard – him appear in the kitchen. Maybe he was getting better with those crutches.

'Quiet, you,' I said, pausing to direct the rebuke at the

shady little shit. 'Hey, whoa! What is this? Young Theodore, making an effort—'

'Shut up,' he said, not so cocky now.

'Just saying, you're looking all right.'

'Don't sound so surprised,' he said, masking his embarrassment with a show of annoyance. 'I always—'

'Yeah,' Claire said. 'You look good.' A small smile, a tight nod – she looked sincere. What's that? No light-hearted yet scathing verbal jab? No doubling down on the Theo needling? Theo looked as shocked as me.

Well now, wasn't this a development... A friendly gesture to keep the peace? An acknowledgement he'd put more than one second of thought or effort into his appearance? Or was the comment a taste of something less platonic to come?

'Uh, thanks,' Theo said, looking more embarrassed than ever.

'You ready to go, then?' Claire said, breezing over my astonishment and Theo's hopeful confusion.

'Yep, yes. Yeah, let's go,' Theo said, looking anywhere but up at me or Claire.

'Behave yourself tonight, Gramps,' Claire said. 'Don't throw out a hip or anything.'

'Yeah, jog on.'

She laughed, opening the door for Theo and closing it behind them both.

'Well, well, well.'

Betty meowed.

'Indeed, Betty,' I said. 'Indeed.'

She watched closely as I transferred the seared chicken pieces back into the roasting dish with the sauce, taking the occasional tentative, half-step forwards each time I lifted a piece across, before sitting back in hopeful anticipation. I rewarded her restraint by dropping another raw scrap that had clung to the tray. And while distracted, I slotted the dish in the oven.

By the time I'd finished the dishes and cleared the kitchen, it was time to baste the chicken. The sauce hadn't thickened much, still running easily as I spooned the sauce from the dish, dousing the chicken pieces for the first of its half-hourly bastings.

I was making good progress, still plenty of time till Arthur showed up. I checked my phone – a smattering of news notifications, promotional emails and messages from friends, but nothing from Arthur. Good, that was good. No last minute cancellation, or fake emergency – not that I'd expected anything like that, but you never knew.

I'd started on tidying up the lounge and vacuuming cat hair off the furniture when someone started banging on the door.

'Mr Bedford!'

I shuddered – what did she want now? My schedule was generous, but it wouldn't accommodate an ear-bending from our landlady if she got stuck in. Perhaps to provide a recap of last night's Residents Committee meeting? Fuck, I hoped not. The meeting minutes hadn't been distributed yet, so she couldn't be checking I'd received them. I'd learnt soon after moving in to acknowledge receipt of the minutes, or Mrs Sheffield would take it upon herself to relay them to you in person, verbally – that had been possibly the longest half hour of my life.

Moments ago both Basil and Betty had been curled up, napping on the back of the couch and the grocery bag, respectively. Upon hearing their owner's voice, they'd leapt up in unison – hackles raised – their wild, feline eyes boring into the front door.

'Miss Thomas! Mr Wright!' she called again, still banging on the door. On hearing her voice again, the cats launched, blurs of ginger and white fur scurrying behind the couch in a clatter of claws.

I'd realised they preferred to stay at ours, but I'd never appreciated the strength of feeling. And for them to react in the same way, when they're otherwise polar-opposite personalities. I shook my head in wonder as I opened the front door before my landlady smashed it down.

'Ah! Good, Mr Bedford.' There she was, looking more agitated than I'd ever seen her, but still doing her best to maintain composure.

'Mrs Sheffield, what can—'

'There's water,' she said, trying to catch her breath, the usual pleasantries abandoned – the situation must be dire. 'There's water dripping through my ceiling, rather quickly in fact.'

'What? Where?'

'In the bathroom – yours is directly above mine,' she said, jabbing a finger in its direction. 'There's a leak in your bathroom.'

'Well, Theo had a shower not long ago,' I said. 'He didn't mention anything wrong.'

'It must be a big leak, surely he'd notice. It's dripping through into my bathroom.'

'Right, OK,' I said. I didn't know what was going on – had Mrs Sheffield been experimenting with her shower head's jet function? Hosed the ceiling by accident? Whatever it was, the sooner she was satisfied the issue wasn't here, the sooner she'd leave. 'Let's investigate then, shall we?'

'Yes, please.'

I led the way down the hall, Mrs Sheffield hot on my heels.

The bathroom door was closed – odd, no one else was here, and we tended to leave the door ajar when unoccupied. I pushed the door, and it budged a little before slamming shut again.

'What…'

'Step aside,' Mrs Sheffield said, shuffling me out of the way before attempting to push the door herself, only to get the same result. 'There's something jammed behind the door. Give it a proper push, young man.'

I couldn't think what might have fallen against the door – most things in the bathroom were either in-built or fixed to the wall. Perhaps someone's washing basket had tipped over?

Mrs Sheffield stepped back to give me room. I braced my feet on the hallway floor, angled my shoulder against the door, and pushed.

That same resistance was still there, but I kept up the pressure and felt some give. As I pushed the door and it swung beyond the edge of the door frame, the resistance dropped away and the door shot open.

With the resistance gone, I stumbled into the bathroom and water up to my shins flooded out.

Chapter 12
Skipping straight to dessert, are we?

I watched my landlady slip and slide down the hallway, screaming as she was carried away on an apartment tsunami.

Water gushed from the shower fittings, a fountain spraying across the bathroom. I braced myself in the door frame as the water poured past my legs. Unable to move for the moment, I looked around at the unfolding disaster when a strip of black caught my eye. Jammed in the gap under the door: Theo's bin bag.

The surge subsided, leaving only a shallow puddle on the bathroom floor. I rushed over to inspect the damage, the water gushing out and drenching me as I approached. The shower fitting had come away from the wall, making the taps useless and leaving the water free to flow. Water sprayed my face when I forced the pipe back into place, making the situation worse. I released the fitting to hang in place and draped the bathmat over the top. This did nothing to fix the plumbing issue, but at least it suppressed the spray and directed the flow straight into the bathtub and down the plug hole.

Mrs Sheffield materialised in the doorway, sopping wet from head to toe, hair like a wild clump of seaweed. All round she looked like a beastly landlady from the deep, come to devour her peasant tenants' first-born as payment.

Before she launched her attack, I said, 'You're right, Mrs Sheffield, there's a leak.' That's step one in appeasing – or at least distracting – the monster: massage their ego, praise their superiority. 'The pipe's burst, but I've got it running into the bathtub now.' The temporary solution. 'We'll need a plumber, did you mention there was one in the building?' And finally, suggest the next step, but let them take control.

She seemed unable to speak for the moment.

'I'll mop up all the water, did you want to call him?' I said, prompting her into action.

'Yes. Yes, I'll give Stephen a call right away,' she said, pulling the hair away from her face and accepting the proffered towel. 'I left my phone downstairs, I'll be right back.' Mrs Sheffield gave my bathmat fix one last look before nodding and leaving.

As soon as she was out I whirled around the flat with the mop and bucket: soaking up the flood, wringing out the mop, and tipping out the bucket. Repeat, repeat, repeat. I couldn't leave any reason for Mrs Sheffield to linger once the plumbing was fixed. If she was satisfied I'd mopped up the water and the floors weren't going to swell or stain, she might leave me alone.

It wasn't long before Mrs Sheffield was back at my door, hair dried and styled, lipstick touched up, and wearing a fresh change of clothes.

'That was quick, Mrs Sheffield.'

'Yes, well, this is a plumbing emergency,' she said. 'We were lucky to have caught Stephen. He was about to head out to a job, but he promised me he'd stop by here first. He should be here shortly.'

'That's great,' I said, making a show of tipping out the last bucket of water. 'I've mopped up the flood, just need to get the tap reconnected.'

'Mm, yes.' She wasn't listening. What was she—

Knock knock knock.

I went to answer the door, but Mrs Sheffield jumped in before me. 'Don't worry, I'll get it,' she said, pausing for a second before opening the front door. 'Ah, Stephen. Thank you ever so much for dropping everything for me to come right over, I really appreciate it.'

'Not at all, Mrs Sheffield,' he said in a voice so low you could almost feel it in your bones. He was a big guy, and in good shape for a bloke in his fifties. I can understand why Mrs Sheffield took a minute to tidy up.

'Don't be silly, you must call me Sharon.' Emphasis on the second syllable – of course – we mustn't forget. 'Have I told you the origins of my name?' she said.

I hovered while our resident lily of the valley recounted her well-rehearsed tale. Stephen's ability to growl acknowledgements at all the right times as he fixed the plumbing was impressive. Though I soon tuned out as Mrs Sheffield droned on, taking great pleasure in handing over tools as Stephen asked for them.

I thought about the wobble in the tap fitting when I'd grabbed it to avoid slipping over last weekend. I knew at the time I'd have to keep an eye on it. Then, this afternoon…

'Don't worry, I caught myself.' Theo had slipped and caught

himself on it too.

Theo would've stripped the bin bag off his leg while drying himself, dropped it on the floor and left the bathroom. Then the stuffed shower fitting finally gave up, bursting apart. Had the rising water floated the bin bag over to plug the gap under the door? To act as a draft stop, effectively sealing the bathroom, watertight? Something like that...

It seemed suspiciously unlikely, as if it were some comically tragic incident designed by some cruel prick determined to ruin my evening... No, I should've seen it coming.

Not that it mattered, not really. It happened and now we just needed it sorted. Mrs Sheffield wanted to minimise the water damage to her place and her rental – understandable. But right now, my only requirements were an operational shower and these two flirty boomers out of the flat.

Stephen had shut off the water and reconnected the pipes by the time our Residents Committee Chairperson had moved on to regaling us with the minutes of yesterday's meeting. She couldn't help herself, what with two non-attending residents as her captive audience. Unfortunately, this now meant I had to pay attention too, murmuring my own responses. As expected though, she'd been out-voted on the relocation of the rubbish drop-off point. No doubt she'd give it a few months and try again.

The plumber stepped back from the shower. 'Should be all done,' he said. 'Just going to turn the water back on, check there's no other leaks and I'll be out of your way.'

'Oh, Stephen. It's no bother,' Mrs Sheffield said. 'You take all the time you need, I'm in no rush.'

Speak for yourself! Arthur was due in under twenty

minutes. I hadn't showered yet, and I needed to finish off the—

'Fuck!' The dinner.

'Mr Bedford, there's no need for such language,' Mrs Sheffield said as I ran to the rescue my chicken.

'Sorry, Mrs Sheffield!' I called over my shoulder as I opened the oven door, waving away the cloud of heat and smoke, and pulled out the dish to check the damage. I'd missed a basting and left it in at full temperature for way longer than it needed. As expected, the chicken pieces had dried right out and the sauce had thickened into something more akin to gravy. I spooned the 'sauce' over the burnt tops of my chicken. Instead of running smoothly down the sides to glisten the chicken, it glooped thickly like I'd dropped lumps of mud on top.

'It's fine, it's fine,' I said to myself. They weren't *that* burnt. And Arthur doesn't know what it's supposed to be like… The situation demanded some creative re-branding. No longer was it 'Braised chicken with chorizo and olives.' No, tonight we were having '*Chargrilled* chicken with chorizo and olives.' Behold, dinner!

I thinned the sauce a little with more white wine, doused the chicken pieces, and returned the dish to the oven at a lower temperature. Not my finest work, but it would have to do.

Now, to evict my landlady and her handyman.

'That's all done then, Sharon,' the plumber said – emphasising the second syllable – as he emerged from the bathroom after completing his checks, with a delighted Mrs Sheffield at his side.

'Thank you very much, Stephen,' she said, hand resting on his arm as they reached the front door. 'We had quite the waterworks going on, didn't we? So wet. Nothing you couldn't handle, though.'

'Any time, but now I must—'

'While I've got you, Stephen,' Mrs Sheffield said, digging her claws into his arm a little more. 'Do you mind checking the bathroom in my apartment? It has the same fittings as this one, which I also own, you see. I want to be sure I'm not about to have the same issue at my place.'

I recognised the man's attempted escape, but like me, he knew when it would be quicker to see to this now. It would take much too long to talk himself out of it, and that would involve promising a visit later. Also not ideal. 'Very well, Sharon,' he said, conceding as I knew he would. 'It'll have to be quick though, I've got that other job I need to get to.'

'Yes, of course. I'll lead the way,' she said. I was hopeful she'd forgotten her reason for being here as she stepped through the front door, but then she turned back, 'Mr Bedford, we'll discuss this later. Perhaps when Miss Thomas and Mr Wright are in.'

I nodded as she closed the door and stalked off with her prey. I'd be anxious of Mrs Sheffield's anticipated advances on his behalf if I wasn't so glad to have them out of the flat. Good on her though – you get it, girl.

I checked the time – less than a quarter of an hour until Arthur was due. That plumbing catastrophe had cannibalised any spare time I'd allowed myself. I flew through the shower. The time left to me meant I couldn't wash as thoroughly as I wanted. Not as comprehensively as a dinner date demanded, anyway – a boy must be prepared for all eventualities. I had to hope the quick version would suffice, and it might not be required anyway. Perhaps Arthur would be more prepared? I was cooking him dinner after all. It was the least he could do… Or maybe he didn't recognise these unspoken rules…

I shook my head. It didn't matter – we'd have a good time, no matter what we got up to. I was drying my hair and gargling mouthwash when I thought I heard something. I stopped to listen—

Knock knock knock.

Shit shit shit. He was here. I spat out the mouthwash and tried to pat my wild, half-dried hair into some order. Wrapping the towel around my waist, I ran towards my room—

Knock knock knock.

No, I'd already left him out there long enough. I couldn't leave him standing around at the front door, feeling awkward and wondering if he had the right place, the right time.

I turned and – wearing nothing but the towel – rushed to open the front door.

And there he was, looking gorgeous, and wielding a bottle of wine in each hand – one red and one white. The look of shock on his face was soon replaced by one of mischief as his eyes tracked up and down my front. 'Skipping straight to dessert, are we?'

I let out a short, sharp bark of a laugh. 'Help yourself to a drink,' I said, waving him in. 'I'll be back out in a minute!'

Chapter 13
What are you insinuating, sir?

Arthur was leaning against the bench when I came out, two generous glasses of red already poured. He faced away from me, idly scrolling through his phone. Though, his attempt at nonchalance was undermined by the jerky side to side movement of his wine glass – the nervous energy was obvious.

The sight of him, though. I gave myself a second to look him up and down now that I wasn't reeling from the shame from being caught in the shower. That body, and even though I couldn't see it right now, the face I hadn't stopped picturing since I'd seen him last. He was adorable, inside and out. To think I'd considered passing, concerned he'd be too much work... What was I thinking?

OK, enough lurking. I headed over. 'High tide is it?'

Arthur jolted and dropped his phone on the bench as he turned to face.

'Wh... what?'

I nodded towards the glasses.

'Oh. Right!' he said, laughing nervously. 'Yes, a little heavy-handed, I suppose. But I'm sure we'll get through it – I'm sorry, I don't even know if you drink wine.' He was horrified at the oversight. 'We only had pints last weekend, so…'

He fizzled out at the scathing look I gave him. That was enough teasing for now – I picked up the glass he'd been buffing the bench top with. 'To generous pours.'

He beamed, 'To generous pours.' We clinked glasses, took a sip and sat in contented silence for a second.

It was very civilised. And the wine was delicious – strong and sweet. I said as much, picking up the bottle. 'And what are we drinking?'

'A Central Otago Pinot noir.'

'And what else have you brought?' I said, picking up the bottle of white.

'A Hawke's Bay Sauvignon blanc. It's an all New Zealand affair tonight.'

'I'll chuck this in the fridge – will go perfect with dinner.' I cringed a little, remembering the state of the burnt chicken.

'Aren't we a pair of wankers?' Arthur said.

I laughed at the unexpected crassness. 'What?'

'Here, discussing wines like a couple of wannabe connoisseurs, pairing them with our meal. All we need now is a wine spittoon and a little bound notebook – the ones with the elastic bands, you know? – to make our tasting notes.'

I dampened down my grin into an expression of stern contemplation, swirling the wine in my glass, giving it a sniff, and holding it up to the light. I brought it down to my nose again, took a sip and sloshed it around my mouth before swallowing.

'There will be no need for spittoons tonight,' I said after completing the theatrics. I looked him in the eyes and said as deadpan as I could manage, 'We mustn't be wasteful. In this house we swallow.'

The look of confusion on his face was swiftly replaced with embarrassment. He chuckled in an attempt to mask the rising colour in his cheeks – it was almost too easy.

'I'll remember that,' he said, taking another slug of wine around his smile.

I couldn't help but laugh again. He'd only been here a few minutes, but I was already enjoying myself.

'Right,' I said, 'you can supervise from there. Perch yourself on a stool and I'll get the last part of dinner going. Should be eating in a little under an hour.' I always appreciated a timeframe – if I was getting hungry, I liked to know when food would be happening and mentally prepare myself.

'Sounds good,' he said, settling on the other side of the bench. 'What have you got left to do?'

'Polenta. The recipe calls for mashed potato, but I thought that might be a bit too homely, thought I'd do something else.'

It was straightforward enough, only requiring a stir every five minutes or so once I'd got it going. With the smells of cooking, the cats soon re-emerged.

'I take it these are your "intermittent flatmates"?' Arthur said as Betty leapt up on the stool beside him.

'Yes,' I said, laughing. 'That one—'

'Let me guess, white fur... This one's Betty?'

'Indeed, it is. Don't judge, we didn't name her.'

'If you're going to be named after someone, you'd do

worse than one of the Golden Girls.'

This boy was a keeper, wasn't he? 'She's always in and around the kitchen at dinner time,' I said. 'Looks like you're tonight's favourite – she must like her chances of schmoozing a treat out of you.'

'How could I say no to that face?' he said, petting Betty on the head. 'And that must mean old gingey over there is Basil?'

'Mean and old is correct,' I said. 'I don't know if I've mentioned, but Basil operates a three-pat-maximum policy. Any more and you'll get a claw.'

'Maybe later, when I'm feeling braver,' Arthur said.

'And don't be lulled into a false sense of security. He'll start purring, but that doesn't mean you can keep petting – you'll still get the claw,' I said. 'Isn't that right, you ornery old bastard?'

Basil hissed in response as he sat in the hallway staring at the front door. He knew we were talking about him. We were still looking in his direction when he got up, stalked over to the door and squatted on the mat.

'You little shit!' I said, rushing out of the kitchen, clapping my hands and stomping until he scarpered across the living room, up the couch and out through the open window. Betty – not happy with all the noise – quickly followed.

I approached the front door and didn't even need to sniff to know I was too late – the acrid odour unmistakable. I rinsed the mat again and hung it to drip dry in the bathroom.

'Sorry about that,' I said as I came back into the kitchen. Arthur had taken the whole fiasco well, not moving from the stool, but his glass was empty. 'Top up?'

'Uh, yeah. Thanks.'

I poured him another large glass, topped myself up and stirred the polenta again. At least this drama hadn't botched another part of dinner. 'He's been doing that lately... I think he's marking his territory, or trying to ward off his owner, Mrs Sheffield.'

'What? Why?'

'The cats hate her. I'm pretty sure they only sneak home to eat, then they're straight back here again. We don't feed them more than the occasional dropped bit of food, and we've got a bowl of water for them. So I think they come here to get away from her, have some peace and quiet. I can't say I blame them... Annoying though, when Basil keeps pissing on the mat. And Betty tries to break into the pantry. She once ate an entire loaf of bread, can't have been good for her. We like having them though – all the pats, none of the responsibility.'

While I finished the polenta, I filled in Arthur on this afternoon's tsunami and warned him about the chicken. Then as I served dinner, and we sat at the table – like proper adults! – we talked about Theo's great downfall and the charged atmosphere in the flat ever since.

'Will they get together, do you think?' he asked as I poured the Sauv.

'Not a chance,' I said, laughing. 'Chalk and cheese, it'd never work.'

'Oh, no. That's got to be awkward. It makes my skin crawl just thinking about it! Do you reckon they'll get back to normal anytime soon?'

'I do hope so, it's been weird around here this week,' I said. 'Tonight's a bit of a test, out for dinner and karaoke, see if things might work again as friends, with feelings all out in the open.'

'A toast,' Arthur said. 'To harmonious living.'

'Cheers!'

We clinked glasses, took a sip with no further fanfare, and started on dinner.

'This tastes amazing,' Arthur said after finishing his first bite, 'if you ignore the burnt bits. And the gluggy sauce. Other than that, ten out of ten.' He smirked.

'Watch it or I'll give it to Betty and feed you some of Theo's pot noodles instead.'

'No! I take it back,' he said. 'It's delicious.' And there he was, back to his earnest, puppy dog eyed self.

'Correct response,' I said. 'Anyway, I've been banging on about my week, how about you? What's been happening? It's been *days* since I saw you.'

Arthur talked about his best friends, Jared – the unlucky-in-love ladies man with a heart of gold – and Richard – the bawdy but lovable bastard with the long-suffering girlfriend, Lucy. Arthur seemed equal parts proud and embarrassed of them. Then he updated me on the regulars at the Sunset Villas retirement home bingo night. It was a joy to see him so animated about his mates and all those crazy pensioners.

'Desmond won the grand prize last week: command of the residents' next big social outing. He's been teasing everyone with tidbits of his plan, and Brenda – Sunset Villas Director – is getting jittery. He's confirmed a few things we *won't* be doing – that is, going to the shopping centre, walking around a park, or visiting some stately garden. But he's given no real hints about what we actually *will* be doing. I tried to get more out of him, but he wasn't having it. He said that as he expected my attendance, I would have to wait and see along with everyone else. Nora's already said she'd save me a seat next to her on the coach. I'm a little worried. She'll have us down the back where she can try and get frisky.'

I choked on my wine when I heard that one. I'd barely contained my amusement during his recap and had mistakenly taken another sip at that point. Arthur made to get up and help – how? – but I waved him away. I'd just recovered when a flash of white shot through the window and leapt onto Arthur's lap.

'Betty! Get down, not during dinner,' I said, shooing her away before she settled in and got her paws up onto the table.

'It's fine, she was OK.'

'No, she knows she can't sit at the dinner table. That little tramp knows what she's up to,' I said, scowling as I sat back down. 'Besides, that lap's mine only tonight.'

He said nothing to that, smiling shyly as he took another mouthful and pulled his chair closer to the table.

'She knows better with us, but probably thought it worth trying her luck on you. The pair of them! On their worst behaviour tonight.'

'And you're not?' Arthur said, smirking again.

This boy! I couldn't pin him down. Swinging wildly from bashful innocence to thinly veiled depravity – I was getting whiplash trying to figure him out. Fun, though – and that's what we're here for, isn't it?

'What are you insinuating, sir?' I said, feigning affront. 'I am the epitome of virtue! Entirely wholesome, inviting you here to provide you a delicious and nutritious meal, with no ulterior motives whatsoever.'

Arthur's smirk grew as I spoke. 'What a pity, and here I

was getting ready to do unseemly things to you.'

It was my turn to feel my neck flush. 'Might be I was lying... Virtue, schmirtue,' I said blowing a raspberry. Oof, how many wines had I had? Not my most articulate or sensible remark.

'Glad to hear it,' Arthur said. 'Top up?'

Sure enough, my glass was empty again. Betty supervised from the floor as Arthur tipped the rest of the bottle into my glass – there hadn't been much left. Two bottles between us and we'd only just finished dinner.

'Never fear, King Arthur,' I said, shooting to my feet. 'I have bubbles in the cellar. We shall not want for refreshment tonight.'

I took the dishes into the kitchen and returned with bubbles and flutes. 'Unfortunately, they were out of Champagne,' I said.

'Who was?'

'The city. The entire kingdom,' I said, sweeping my arm wide. 'Not a drop of Champagne to be seen at the cheap end of the wine isle. Instead, tonight we'll be sampling the supermarket's finest, low-cost, discount fizzy wine.' My budget couldn't accommodate the real deal, even for a nice date.

'Goodness,' Arthur said. 'Gabriel, you shouldn't have! You know that's my favourite.'

'Well,' I said, handing over the bottle as we moved to the living room, 'will you do the honours and pop my cork?'

Arthur gaped as he accepted the bottle. 'If I wasn't already half-cut, I'd be embarrassed for you.'

'Good that I've been plying you with your own wine all night then, isn't it?'

'Absolutely. Well played.' Arthur untwisted the wire

cage, then resting the bottle on his upper thigh, he worked off the cork. 'I'm almost there, are you close?'

'Yeah, go for it!'

The bottle produced a loud, crisp pop, accompanied by a 'Yeow!' from Arthur.

'And you had the cheek to be embarrassed on my behalf?' I said, laughing along with his spectacle, not so much suggestive as outright obscene. Who was I kidding, I was on board – obviously.

'All right, let me fill you up,' Arthur said with a smirk.

'Oh, yes.' I held the glasses as he poured. 'Keep going, that's it.'

'Mm, yes. Hear that effervescence as it whooshes into the glass.' His expression had shifted, dead serious now.

'Like the stirring of leaves in a crisp, autumn breeze,' I said, equally impassive.

'The bubbles bursting and babbling – quite lively – now fading to a gentle hiss,' Arthur said, maintaining his aloof facade while setting the bottle down on the coffee table. He held up his glass to the light, 'A nice straw gold colour. Wonderful.'

'The brilliance, the clarity, the play of the light as I behold the bubbles rising to the surface.'

'Hmm... These bubbles, could they possibly be... Too big?'

'I wondered that myself,' I said, squinting at my glass. 'Perhaps a little too coarse, not as fine as one would like.'

'A pity, not their finest vintage.'

'Though, I suppose we can endure the bottle.'

'We shall, as you say, endure.'

'Perhaps...' I said, holding up a finger then taking a gulp, gargling and swallowing. 'Yes, it would make a fine mouthwash. Start one's day off on the right foot.'

Arthur, who had been snorting in his attempts to keep his amusement in check, finally let loose. With him gone, I couldn't hold myself back any longer. We were crying and roaring with laughter as we dropped onto the couch. One of us would be settling down, before making the mistake of looking at the other which set us off all over again. Basil had made an appearance on the back of the couch at some point, one eye twitching open in annoyance whenever we got going.

Once our fits had diminished to mere chuckles, I said, 'So, to what shall we toast?'

Arthur looked at me, his expression convincingly sober. 'I propose we raise a toast,' he said, lifting his glass, 'to dick.'

I barked out a laugh and raised my glass to his, 'To dick!'

'Amen.'

We snickered some more as we settled into the couch. Then the laughter faded into companionable silence. I watched as Arthur sipped his bubbles. He seemed at ease this evening – no doubt the booze helped. But he appeared comfortable, just us two – not at all like at the cafe where he'd clammed up and become self-conscious. I knew he'd still be on edge next time we were out in public together, hyper-conscious of nearby strangers assuming we were a couple of homos. One day he'd realise most people wouldn't notice, and if they did, most wouldn't care.

The next step was for us to get out, and for Arthur to be out. He'd learn to grow less bothered by it all. It'd never vanish completely – there would always be those loutish lads who felt it was their duty to teach us a lesson, but they were in the minority around these parts. And we couldn't let them scare us back into the closet along with the camel corduroy trousers and check shirts.

No, I'd take my time with this guy. There was no hurry to whip his gay training wheels off. We'd have him in skimpy swimwear and a leather harness soon enough... Or maybe not – we didn't need to go full pride parade if we didn't want to.

But the real sign would be him asking me out, properly. Not a drink at the pub with mates, not a morning-after brunch with a 'friend' where he hadn't realised at first how it would look to others at the cafe... A proper date. Just us, going out somewhere where it's clear that we were there *together*. I'm not talking wedding bells, but I think this thing we had going on was more than a casual shag. We were becoming more than friends, but I had to leave the next step up to Arthur – I couldn't pile on the pressure by asking him out myself... One day he might pluck up the courage.

Betty leaping onto my lap brought me back to the present. Without thinking, I gave her a pat, immediately firing up the purr machine.

'I see how it is,' Arthur said. 'You'll give anyone back rubs these days, won't you?'

'Hah! Your massage was only an excuse for me to get my hands on you,' I said with a sly grin. 'I should've thanked Susan for that opportunity when I saw her last weekend...'

'Now that I think about it, you never gave me that massage you promised me at my birthday drinks.'

'We both know that was just an excuse to ditch Richard and Jared. Lovely as they are, once your gayness was out in the open I had other ideas about how I wanted to spend the rest of your birthday.'

'You selfish bastard,' Arthur said, faux indignant. 'First, you take over my birthday, then you take me home with the promise of a nice back massage, and all I got was hot, toe-curling sex. I feel shafted!'

I couldn't help but smile at that. 'Literally.'

Arthur was biting down on his own smile. 'Well! If you get Betty, I'll have Basil,' he said, setting down his glass and turning to kneel on the cushions. He reached for the ball of ginger fur on the back of the couch.

'I wouldn't do that if I were you,' I said in my sternest, most matronly voice.

'Such selfish behaviour – I've had enough!' Arthur said, sticking out his chin in mock defiance. 'I will do as I bloody well please.' He lifted Basil, turned back to sit, and plopped the cat on his lap. 'See! Now, how about—'

And that's when Basil attacked.

I saw the signs but wasn't fast enough to intervene. He unsheathed his claws as I leapt to pull him off Arthur's lap. Betty scrambled away as I launched, her claws digging into my thighs through my jeans. The wine flung from my glass, dousing Arthur and Basil as the cat took a swipe at his forearm and clambered up his chest, over his shoulder, onto the back of the couch and out the open window.

I landed awkwardly in Arthur's lap, elbowing him in the stomach and making the whole situation worse. Arthur was shaking now. It wasn't until I'd backed away that I realised he was laughing in between bouts of coughing. 'All you had to do was ask,' he said, still laughing.

'What?'

'If you wanted to climb into my lap,' he said. 'Though, a little less elbow next time, hmm?'

'How about now?'

'Sure,' he said, 'though I am a little sticky from your wine.'

'So you are,' I said. His shirt was covered in a big dark splotch. 'We'd better get you out of that top.'

'If you must,' Arthur said. He went to take off his shirt, and that's when I saw—

'You're bleeding!' Blood was smeared up his arm – Basil's vengeance. 'Bring it here.'

'It's fine,' he said as he laid out his arm on the couch.

'You stay right there.' I grabbed the first aid kit from under the sink and wiped his forearm with an antiseptic wipe.'

'See!' he said. 'Not so bad.'

He was right – it only took one of the medium-sized plasters to cover it up.

'Susan would be impressed,' Arthur said, glowing.

'Hah,' I said, packing the kit away, 'it was hardly a—'

Arthur kissed me and I froze. It was as if he'd lit a fuse, the anticipation coursing through my body, sparked by only the touch of his lips. I abandoned packing up the first aid kit, leant in and kissed him back. We were locked in place, our hands soon exploring the contours of each other's bodies with increasing urgency.

After a moment Arthur pulled back and said, 'Shall we take this to the bedroom?'

I just wanted to keep going right here, not waste any more time – I said as much.

Arthur grinned, pushing me down onto the couch, straddling my hips as he pulled his wine-stained shirt over his head and flung it across the room. Watching his stomach, chest and arms flex and contort as he completed the manoeuvre sent another jolt through me. 'OK, right here,' he said, looking down at me on my back like he was about to devour me.

I couldn't look away – he was gorgeous. But he didn't give me long to stare before his lips were back on mine. Then, without breaking contact, he had his hands under my shirt, pulling it up.

I was so engrossed that I didn't hear the clomp of crutches or heels in the hallway, or the clatter of keys outside the apartment. The first I knew something was up was when Theo bellowed, 'Gramps! We're baaaaack!'

Chapter 14
We'll have to see, won't we?

'Claire, they're going at it!' screamed Theo from the doorway. 'On the couch!'

In our scramble to extricate ourselves from each other, Arthur kneed me in the crotch, causing me to curl in on myself in agony, head-butting him in the process. By the time we'd both recovered enough to sit up, Theo had plodded over to us, flanked by an amused Claire.

'What are you two doing back so early?' I said as I pulled my shirt back on. The best defence is offence, right?

'Oh, ho ho. Good try, old man,' Claire said, waggling her finger at me as she stalked back and forth, emphasising her words with the clack of her heels – how much had they drunk? 'You boys have had the house to yourselves all evening.'

'Yeah, get a room, old man! Not our fault you're so slow getting his kit off,' Theo said. But where the booze had animated Claire, sharpening her every word, Theo just slurred his together in one indecipherable ramble. He nodded at Arthur then, 'Nice to meet you, by th' way.'

'You've already met him, Theo,' I said.

'What? No, I haven't,' Theo said.

'At the hospital.'

'No,' Theo said. 'Even I would remember a hunk of man meat like *that*.'

'Mm,' Claire said, lips pursed in appraisal as she too ogled Arthur. 'Anyway, I have to agree with Theo, about your sluggishness, that is. I'd have had him bouncing around on my bed *hours* ago.'

'Hey! Arthur's *right here*,' I said, shifting to put myself between him and them, obscuring their view. He was still shirtless – I should've given him mine. That would've been the chivalrous thing to do.

'Yeah, hey! I'm right here too,' Theo said to Claire, almost losing a crutch as he gestured to himself. 'Is all this beef not enough for you?'

Claire turned to humour Theo, making a performance of ogling him as well. 'We'll see, won't we?' she said before planting a big kiss on him. And not a friendly, drunken play-flirt kiss on the cheek, but a full-on pash on the lips, the type that came with a promise of more bumping and grinding in the very near future.

'Wh—'

'So, Gramps…' Theo said, looking a little sheepish now. 'Claire and I, we got to talking at the karaoke—'

'Turns out I'd never given this adorable dweeb a chance,' Claire said.

'Dweeb?' Theo said, blinking in outrage.

'And once I'd gotten over his big, stupid proclamation last weekend, and considered what my life would be like without this goober—'

'Fuck's sake,' Theo said, shaking his head in disbelief.

'—I realised I had feelings for him too.' She smiled at him then. 'I didn't want to regret not seeing if there was something here. So I thought, why not? What's the worst that could happen?'

'Well...' I said. 'I can think of a few—'

'The more vodka lemonades I had, the more convinced I became—'

'Ah, see,' I said, 'Claire, there it is. Your reasoning, not up to your usual high standards and—'

'Gramps, you boring old stiff. You wouldn't know, but there are only so many drinks you can down and eighties power ballads you can belt out on a school night,' she said, clacking back and forth again on her heels as she jabbed her finger in my direction. 'I *reasoned* that coming home would be the most *sensible* thing to do. We've already stopped to have doner kebabs, soak up most of the booze. And now,' she said, turning to smile at Theo, 'we're going to my bedroom to sweat out the rest, aren't we Theo?'

'Yeah,' he said in awe, like he couldn't believe his good fortune.

'Gross...' It took me a moment to recover from that one. Then, putting on my best no-nonsense voice, I said, 'As the elder of the flat, I propose we all retire to our *own* bedrooms. And sleep off the booze instead.'

'Shall I call Arthur a ride, then?' Claire said, eyebrows almost up to her hairline.

'Uh, no,' I said, unexpectedly turned around. 'No, I meant you two. You two should... should go to your own rooms.'

'You're sending us to our rooms, are you? Meanwhile, you'll be in your room shagging King Arthur, hmm?' Claire was getting fired up now, and she had a point. 'This *reeks* of double standards. You are not my mother, and you will not tell me what I can or cannot do.'

With that, she grabbed Theo and shunted him towards her room. He righted himself after an initial stumble and then moved at a pace I didn't know he was capable of, even pre-injury.

'Sorry!' I called out after them. 'I didn't mean—'

She flipped me off and slammed the bedroom door behind her.

'That... that didn't come out how I intended,' I said, turning to Arthur. 'I'm sorry about all that.'

'Don't worry about it,' he said, smiling as he put his hand on my knee. 'They'll have cooled down by tomorrow. Either they'll be fine – happy days! – or it'll go terribly and they'll realise you were right. No matter what, you'll be here to congratulate them, or support them through that gnarly awkwardness and awful hurt feelings.'

I sighed. 'You're right.'

His hand slid up my thigh. 'So, now the kids have gone to bed, maybe we should, too?'

'Wow,' I said, screwing up my face and laughing. 'OK. It's time we got you out of all these clothes.'

Arthur gave me a quick kiss and then jumped up, pulling me with him. 'Mustn't get carried away on the couch again.'

I laughed and scooped up the bottle of bubbles and our glasses. 'In case we get thirsty,' I said as I led him towards my bedroom.

'Must keep our fluids up. Stay hydrat—'

Knock knock knock.

'What the fuck is it now?' I said without realising I'd opened my mouth, beyond frustrated by now. Didn't these people realise I had things – that is, Arthur – to do? I took a deep breath, handed the bubbles and glasses to Arthur, said I'd be right back, then went to get rid of our late night caller.

I unlocked and opened the door to see Mrs Sheffield in her cosy, quilted dressing gown which clashed with her furious expression and bleary, bloodshot eyes. 'What—'

'Mr Bedford, do you have a lady staying over tonight?' she said, trying to peer over my shoulder.

'What? No, why?' I understood what she meant, but if she asked dumb questions, I'd give her dumb answers.

'Heels! Clattering around on my nice wooden floors. First, this afternoon you flood my floors with your little bathroom fiasco, and now – at this hour! – flagrant disregard of the tenancy agreement – which you signed! – which expressly prohibits high-heeled shoes from being worn on the property.'

'I'm sorry Mrs Sheffield, you're mistaken,' I said, knowing full well it was Claire's heels. Claire – normally so cautious on the rare occasions she wore heels – was pissed at me for bossing her around and had probably been more stompy than usual. 'That must have been Theo you heard. He was a little drunk when he got home, and not at his best with his crutches. You recall he broke his leg last week? I'll ask him to try and walk more softly in the future, but it should only be a few more weeks until he can do away with the crutches.'

Mrs Sheffield was frothing by this point. 'It was not those crutches I heard – it was heels! And I know it wasn't Miss Thomas, that girl doesn't have the first clue how to dress nicely. Traipsing around in boys' clothes half the time. And what's she studying? Rocks?'

'What? She's studying geology, though I don't see

what—'

'Geology! Yes, hardly a suitable career for a woman—'

'OK! Mrs Sheffield, that's enough,' I said, having lost patience with this troll. 'Theo has gone to bed, so there will be no more clomping tonight. I will speak with him in the morning.' I held up a finger to interrupt my landlady as she inhaled, no doubt preparing to launch into some other inane verbal onslaught. 'And if you weren't so wilfully oblivious, you'd know I would never bring a *lady* home to stay the night.' Stepping back so she could see through to a shirtless Arthur holding our bubbles and flutes, I said, 'As you can see I have a *man* staying over tonight. And, as you can also see, he's not wearing heels.'

This had the desired effect of shutting her up, embarrassing her and giving her something to mull over.

'You can rest easy tonight. By the time you get back to your apartment, even Arthur and I won't be walking around on the floors anymore because – before you interrupted us – we were on our way to bed.'

She was still goldfishing as I apologised again for the noise, wished her a good night, and closed the front door.

I turned to Arthur. 'Sorry about *that*. Wow, I feel like all I'm doing tonight is apologising.'

He smiled. 'That's OK, I won't forget this evening in a hurry.'

'Next time,' I said as I led Arthur to my room, 'we're going to your place.'

'We'd still have to contend with Patty at my place.'

'Compared to my landlady, flatmates and the cats, Patty seems manageable.'

Arthur set the bottle and glasses on my desk, gave the room a once-over and turned to me. 'Such a small room for such a big boy,' he said, his mouth twitching in amusement.

'I'm sure you'll fit,' I said, smirking in return.

'Only one way to find out,' Arthur said, throwing himself onto the bed.

I was on him in seconds, picking up right where we left off – finally. I mean, talk about a frustrating, blue-balling series of false starts – you wouldn't read about it.

We were pressed against each other, head to toe, fully clothed except for Arthur's shirt. It had taken us this long to get to this point, I wasn't about to rush things now.

I had one hand under his neck, the other in his hair. He had his hands under my shirt, running up my back. And my mouth locked on his – no time for chat.

It wasn't long before we abandoned any intentions of taking this at a relaxed pace. I was about to start working my way down when I felt my crotch vibrate. And again. I lurched back onto my haunches, kneeling with one leg either side of Arthur's.

'For fuck's sake, my phone,' he said, reaching into his pocket. Then, without checking the caller, he dropped it on the bedside table and pulled me back down on top of him. We smiled against each other lips as his phone stopped vibrating and we got back to it.

It mustn't have been ten seconds before it started vibrating again. This time, without breaking our kiss, Arthur lifted his hand off me, slapped it on the bedside table, and silenced the call in one fluid motion – impressive.

I wrapped my arms around him and rolled us over so I was on my back and he was on top – I wanted to get the rest of those clothes off. We were still kissing as I worked at his belt, and his phone started vibrating a third time. I grabbed his hand as he reached out to silence it again. 'You'd better answer it,' I said, wanting nothing less than the complete opposite. 'Doesn't sound like they're giving up.'

Arthur sighed and clambered off me to sit on the side of the bed. 'It's Richard,' he said, sounding confused and concerned. 'He never calls.'

'Go on, answer it,' I said, sitting up beside him.

'Richard, what's up?' he said.

I couldn't hear what was said, but he sounded excited, not upset. Then realising I was eavesdropping, I backed away, intending to wait out in the lounge when Arthur's free hand clamped on my arm, pulling me back beside him as he listened to his friend.

'Yeah... And?... What did – yeah?' Arthur sounded excited – good news then. 'Well, shit! Congrats, man. That's amazing!... What, really?... Of course! Uh, maybe give that some more thought... What? So soon?... Fine, yes, of course... Yeah, I'm at Gabriel's tonight... He's right here... Mm hmm, OK...' Less excited now, more uncertain. 'Uh, you kinda did... Yeah, like, right in the middle,' Arthur said, looking at me with an embarrassed grimace. 'Yes, that would be good... Really pleased for you, man!... Yes, yes, I'll let you know... I love you too mate, but don't call again tonight or I'll gut you... Yes, I knew you'd understand... Hah! OK yeah, fuck off.'

He hung up and dropped the phone on the bedside table. I looked at him expectantly.

'Richard and Lucy are engaged!' Arthur said, buzzing with excitement. 'Lucy just proposed. She always said she would, but Richard didn't believe her, thought she was winding him up. He was so pleased though when she asked, and he said yes!'

'That's great news!' Arthur's delight was infectious and I

couldn't help grinning right back at him.

'And, the wedding is in two weeks.'

'What? Two weeks, what's the hurry? Did she get him pregnant?'

Arthur laughed. 'No, they called up a venue Lucy had in mind, to get information. They've had a last-minute cancellation, otherwise the next available slot isn't for nearly two years. They didn't want to wait, so two weeks it is.'

'Wow.'

'And! And he's asked both me and Jared to be his joint Best Men. To tell us apart, he's proposed Jared be his Best Breast Man and I be his Best Butt Man... I told him to work on it.'

I couldn't help but laugh at that. 'Well, shit. I know what we need,' I said, grabbing the bubbles. 'A toast! There's got to be some fizz left in this...' I poured us a glass each – not as effervescent as earlier, but it'd do.

Arthur raised his and said, 'To Richard and Lucy! The most unexpectedly perfect couple and the last I thought would get married.'

'To Richard and Lucy,' I said, clinking our glasses and taking a slug.

Arthur downed his in one gulp and set his glass down. He looked nervous and wary, like all the wind had gone out of his sails.

'What – what is it?' I said, putting my glass aside, only half drunk.

'Uh... Well... You know I've only recently come out...' Arthur was falling over his words and leaving long, drawn out pauses as he stared at his hands. I wasn't sure where he was going with this, and I wanted nothing more than to help him along, but he needed to do this himself, at his own pace. 'Well, I said I wanted to take it slow, and you were great about it. Even though I know it must be frustrating for you... But I really like you. And I think you feel the same. So, uh... Do you... do you want to come to the wedding with me?' At this point he looked up at me, making eye contact for the first time since he'd started rambling. 'As my plus-one? As my boyfriend?'

I was speechless for a second before Arthur jumped right back in.

'You don't have to! It's only a couple of weeks away, I'm sure you already have plans. And we hardly know each other. We—'

I shut him up with a kiss, then pulled back and said, 'I would love to come with you as your plus-one... As your boyfriend.'

If I thought I'd seen this boy's face light up before, it was nothing on what I saw now. Then it abruptly dimmed, 'Are you sure, though?'

'Of course I am,' I said. 'Are you?'

'Yes!'

I smiled. 'Prove it.'

He grinned wildly back at me before latching on to my lips, pushing me back onto the bed and tearing at my shirt and jeans.

About bloody time.

Thank you for reading

I hope you enjoyed the story. If you did, please tell your friends – personal recommendations are the best! Also please consider leaving reviews on Amazon and Goodreads. This is important in making my work more visible to other readers – each review gives the books a little boost in the charts, meaning others are more likely to stumble across them.

For my latest updates and a free short story you can join the mailing list on my website: www.gbralph.com. You can also find my other stories there, and links to my social media if you'd like to drop me a message – I'd love to hear from you!

But before you go...

The story continues...

**Over and Out
Rise and Shine – Book Three**

A gay romantic comedy novella about coming out, coming apart, and coming together.

Arthur and Gabriel both lead busy lives, and now they've got a shotgun wedding to attend. Their first event as a couple – that is, if they last that long.

Arthur's adopted grandparents have dragged him out on their mystery day trip. But the mischievous oldies are more interested in meddling with his love life.

Meanwhile, Gabriel is living the big city life. Scrambling to cram in study, work shifts, and a social life, now he's determined to pursue something else: his new man.

With a baffling series of events conspiring to keep them apart, can they make it work?

Over and Out is the sequel to Slip and Slide, but this time, we're not only in Arthur or Gabriel's head, we're flip-flopping between the two! Everyone gets a turn. Such a versatile arrangement – it's only fair.

Want to slip straight in?

Grab yourself a copy of *Over and Out*:
www.gbralph.com/over-and-out

Or, read a sneak preview right now...

Chapter 1
Who's to say this won't be the same?

ARTHUR

'Bingo!'

Desmond sprung up, sending his collapsible chair flying backwards. The abrupt manoeuvre set off a chorus of alarm from the dabbers behind him. He ignored the protests in his eager shuffle to the front of the makeshift bingo hall which belied his advanced years.

'I knew it – could feel it in these old bones, you see. Here it is, Mr Wonka,' he said, waving the card in the air before slamming it down on my table, 'the golden ticket.'

'And how sure are we today?' I said, well aware of Desmond's tendency to stir up trouble when he'd decided a game had dragged on too long. On occasions I caught him fabricating a win, he would brush it off, blaming the error on senility. Though, we all knew he was still in complete control of his full set of marbles. He didn't help his case when he coupled these announcements with a mischievous wink.

'I trust you'll find everything's in order,' the old man said with a look of mock indignation. Then when I didn't respond right away he added, 'You doubt my sincerity, young man?'

'I would never,' I said, smiling at Desmond's theatrics.

'And while you're busy validating my honour – unimpeachable, I assure you – I thought I may take this opportunity to remind my fellow geriatrics of tomorrow's outing?'

I waved him on as I checked his numbers. Though nominally in charge of bingo night – calling the numbers, checking tickets, distributing prizes – I still saw myself as a guest. Sunset Villas was their home and my weekly appearances didn't give me the clout to refuse a resident, especially one such as Desmond – he'd do as he pleased. And, considering my attendance was expected for tomorrow's outing, I was intrigued to see what was planned. I hadn't had the heart to turn down the invite. Besides, Desmond assured everyone it would be an entertaining day out, and I had plenty of leave owing at work.

'All right, quiet down you old coots,' Desmond said to the seated bingo players. 'I know you're all *dying* to know what tomorrow's outing will entail. Now, I won the right to organise this outing and I've put a fair bit of planning into it, so don't you go knocking boots with old Mr Reaper in your dreams tonight – you'll be no good to us on the slab.'

This comment was met with huffs of disapproval and superstitious hand movements from around his audience.

'Besides,' Desmond continued, 'it might be rather

dispiriting for those of us with one foot still soundly out of the grave. So, if you're feeling anxious, perhaps you can borrow a couple of Maud's heavy-duty pills to get you through the heightened anticipation.'

I glanced up from checking Desmond's ticket to see Maud looking her usual serene self, hands clasped on the designer handbag resting on her knees and nodding along vacantly to Desmond's spiel. She didn't play bingo, but enjoyed being amongst the action – that's what I presumed anyway, seeing as she was here week after week.

'Come now, Dez.' That was Nora, our resident heckler. 'Just tell us, you old tease.' She was as bad as Desmond when it came to stirring, and a shameless flirt to boot. I'd have to supervise her, determined as the old girl was to have her way with me. She might try her luck tomorrow, fuelled by the day's adventures and unfamiliar surroundings.

'Calm yourself, Nora – you'll find out on the coach. Which – everyone listening? – will leave from out the front at nine on the dot. So, fire up those walking frames nice and early because latecomers will be left—'

'Will Arthur be joining us?' Nora said, cutting across Desmond.

'Yes, I believe he will,' he said, turning to me for confirmation.

I paused, then nodded – if I wasn't committed before, I was now. Nora smiled in return. She was plotting something and wasn't concerned if I knew.

'And what about this secret lover, hmm?' Nora wasn't even pretending to direct her query to Desmond anymore. 'Will we be introduced tomorrow, too? Or do you plan to keep this mystery beauty squirrelled away forever?'

'I – uh – no,' I said. 'It's just, you know, much too short notice. University and work commitments – another shift at the driving range – all that. And we hardly know each other, not ready to go introducing h—'

'What's it been, my boy – a fortnight?' Gerry said, cutting off my rambling in his warm, deep voice. I was grateful for the interruption.

'Uh, yeah.' Two weeks… was that all? It felt like a lot longer since we'd first run into each other – literally.

'There you have it, Nora. The kids are still getting acquainted with each other. When I was a young buck courting my Ava, I certainly wasn't willing to share her with my grandmother's friends on a geriatric day trip. We had other, more *youthful* ideas about how we wanted to spend our time together.' A few titters from the listening players met this remark. 'So, Nora, you let the boy take his time. We'll get to meet young Arthur's special someone soon enough.' He winked at me, and I smiled my cautious gratitude in return.

Gerry always had my back, though I remember being terrified of him as a child. Even now I could understand why, at first glance, you might write him off as a grumpy old prick. I didn't know it at the time, but it was Gerry dressed as Santa Claus the year I flat out refused to hop on Santa's lap. I'd been rehearsing my proclamation of impeccable virtue and preparing to recite my well-rehearsed Christmas wish list. But the moment I saw Santa, I lost it – throwing a tantrum and refusing to make my in-person request. Instead, I remember crossing my fingers extra hard on the journey home and hoping my letter to the North Pole would be enough to convince Big Red I deserved to be well rewarded.

Momentarily put out, Nora was quick to recover. 'Well then, looks like I have you all to myself tomorrow, young Mr Fenwick.' She paused, as if a thought had just come to her. 'Probably best to keep your lovers separate, anyway. I hate to think what might happen if we had to compete for your affections. I am perhaps a little more mature than your other paramour. In general, I am averse to admitting such a thing, but in this instance I think it's an asset. I expect I am somewhat more cool-headed as an experienced woman of the world, so can share a man without being overwhelmed by the green-eyed monster. It would be hypocritical of me to have such counterproductive feelings when I also do not restrict myself to one suitor.'

It seemed Nora's campaign to lure me to her bed was far from over. And neither had her determination to rid herself of any love-rivals diminished, despite her words to the contrary. I maintained a polite grimace, not trusting myself to respond.

'Anything else, Nora?' Desmond said, staring down my unabashed admirer with impatience. 'Or are you *quite* done?'

Nora quirked a cheeky smirk and shrugged – she would speak whenever she pleased and there was nothing anyone could do about it.

Desmond must have realised this was as good as he'd get, so he continued. 'Our esteemed Dictator – hah, slip of the old tongue.' He chuckled to himself. 'Our esteemed *Director* took some convincing in approving this outing. We all know how hard-nosed our dear Ms Myles can be, but even she could not help but succumb to my faultless reasoning and relentless charm.'

Nora scoffed.

Desmond spoke louder, 'She did, however, insist I pass on this.' He reached into his trousers—

Nora wailed. 'Nobody wants to see that wrinkled old thing!'

He grumbled as he pulled a slip of paper from his pocket and cleared his throat with more fanfare than I expected was strictly necessary. 'Ms Myles requests attendees wear comfortable shoes and a jacket, bring a bottle of water and a travel mug or coffee flask—'

'What about lunch?' Nora said.

'—but there's no need to bring food as the kitchens will prepare lunch,' Desmond said, pointedly ignoring Nora as he shoved the paper back into his pocket, then smiled. 'Don't forget to eat your porridge tomorrow morning – you'll be needing the energy. And I promise you'll be getting some real *bang* for your *buck*.'

Desmond grinned like the cat that got the cream and headed for his seat, apparently having forgotten why he'd come up in the first place.

'Desmond,' I said, calling after him. 'Don't forget your prize.' Turns out the old scoundrel's win was legitimate – this time, anyway. I handed over his winnings: a selection of biscuits in a round tin with pastoral scenes shown on the sides and the lid.

He looked at his prize, appearing reluctant. I could understand the reaction. It was the kind of gift a parent might buy on behalf of their child to gift their grandfather on Father's Day, along with the card lovingly crafted at kindergarten. One could appreciate the effort put into making the card – 'Such interesting colour choices, my boy. And you've certainly used a substantial amount of glue – this painted macaroni won't be coming off anytime soon, will it? Well done.' But no one *actually* enjoyed those nasty, dry biscuits – did they? Not when you could buy a far superior biscuit from the supermarket for a fraction of the price. And what was one to do with yet *another* tacky biscuit tin? There were only so many sewing kits one household could contain. Most likely it'd be stacked on the ever-growing pile under the stairs or in the garage… It's the thought that counts though, right? But let's be honest, they could've thought of something else.

That's when I saw Desmond's expression slowly shift from dubious to delighted. He reached to claim his prize and said, 'This will do perfectly, I think. I have just the job in mind for this handsome tin.'

Suspicious… I almost tried to take it back, knowing he couldn't possibly be up to any good with a reaction like that. I returned the balls to the cage as Desmond returned to his seat and tried not to worry about his scheming.

Perhaps I could see Maud about one of those pills to calm myself for tomorrow? No, better not – they were potent little beasts. I couldn't be falling asleep on the coach – who knows what might become of me.

'OK,' I said, cutting across the hushed conversations which had broken out around the room. 'Next up we have a game of Two Lines – you know the rules. And the prize for this round is a lovely bottle of port.'

A flurry of excitement met this news, and I noticed Charles and Nora were now looking particularly determined. 'All right, folks' – I clapped my hands once – 'eyes down.'

The roomful of pensioners hunched over their tables, laser-focused as I opened the cage to grab the first ball.

'13, unlucky for some. 13.' Gladys gave her ticket a

triumphant yet vicious dab – seems she wanted the tipple too and was off to a good start. Otherwise, the room was filled with frustrated murmurs, everyone else disappointed to miss that auspicious first call. Though, it was a rather ominous ball to pull at the outset.

'32, buckle my shoe. 32.' Dabbers remained hovering over tickets to a susurration of tuts – another uncommon number this round it seemed.

'25, duck and dive. 25.' I saw several satisfied jabs – redemption! Perhaps this game might go their way after all.

'17, dancing queen. 17.' At this I heard a few cheers, an 'Oh, yeah!' and a 'Mamma Mia!' Sounds like we were back on track.

Then I pulled out the next ball… and winced.

Perhaps the punters would be too wrapped up in ABBA and wouldn't notice if I sneaked this ball back in? It was absolutely against the rules, but I think I would be forgiven in this instance… thanked, even. About to make my move, Charles – always the gentlemen, but much too observant – innocently enquired about the next number. There was nothing for it, I had to do it…

'85, staying alive. 85.'

Right on cue, Desmond was back out of his seat for the second time tonight – and tap-tap-tapping a rhythm on Gerry's near-bald head. The gruff old softy was trying to bat his fellow resident away when Desmond slid into the aisle and swaggered towards me at the front. He crooned in falsetto the opening lines to the Bee Gees hit as he strutted – as much as an octogenarian can – around the punters, blowing air-kisses to the ladies and nodding to the gents. He hit the chorus with even more gusto – nobody on the Sunset Villas grounds in any doubt about Desmond's intention to be staying alive.

Inside I was groaning, but I played along, pretending to be amused. He'd made a full lap of the room – treating each and every attendee to a little personal boogie and a line or two of the classic disco tune – before he settled back down in his seat.

'Thank you, Dez. That was a treat, as always.' I could've changed the call – there's plenty that rhymes with 'five' – but Desmond was liable to launch a one-man riot if he missed his moment in the spotlight.

'My pleasure, young man,' he said, breathless from exertion as he eased himself back into his seat. 'I'm not as spry as I once was, but I couldn't let down my fans.' His so-called fans were quick to shush the old troublemaker – they had a game to get on with.

I drew the next ball from the cage. '63, tickle me. 63.' Nora pursed her lips and gave me a wink. That woman was something else, any chance she got.

The next series of calls passed without incident – tension building and hands shaking with anticipation as dabbers marked out more numbers. A few contenders squirmed in their seats now – I suspected each were a single call away from victory.

'29, rise and shine. 29.'

'Bingo!'

Sure enough. Charles beamed as he rose, gracious in his acknowledgement of his fellow residents' polite applause. Gladys joined in the civilised round of congratulations, even though it was clear she'd had her heart set on that bottle of port. Nora, though – never shy to let her feelings be known – sat back with her arms crossed and a scowl plastered across her wrinkled face.

'Come now, Nora.' I wasn't willing to let her get away without a little ribbing, considering how much she dished out. 'I'm sure Charles will share a glass if you ask nicely.'

At that, she remembered herself, rearranging her face into her signature look of mischievous delight, which she turned on me. 'Such a cheeky young man. Were you not taught to respect your elders?' she said with eyebrows raised. 'What a naughty boy, I think I must discipline you myself. It would be irresponsible of me not to address this transgression. No, that would not do… I'll expect you in my apartment after bingo for your first lesson.'

I should've known better than to try and wind up Nora – that wily old girl could turn any situation to her advantage. Though fortune shone on me then in the form of Charles arriving with his alarmingly comical moustache to present his ticket and claim his prize. And so I was saved from concocting yet another excuse to escape Nora's proposition.

'This will do nicely, I think,' Charles said as he picked up his bottle of port and returned to his seat.

Our third and final game was uncharacteristically civilised, with Elspeth taking it out, announcing her triumph with somewhat more restraint and decorum than today's first two winners.

'Young Mr Fenwick, I do believe I have "bingo",' she said, making it clear she was only uttering such a foolish word as she was obliged to do so. She took her time raising herself from her seat, patting down her floral blouse and adjusting her already perfectly positioned pearls before making her way to the front.

Our highest-nosed resident placed her ticket on the table before clasping her hands together on her skirt to await my inspection.

'Mrs Abbington, you do indeed hold the winning ticket.' She nodded in affirmation, her blue rinse bouffant hair moving not an inch as she accepted her voucher. 'Your prize is a double pass to any of the local theatre company's matinee performances this season. I saw somewhere their next production is Macbeth, a modern interpretation set in the world of property investment.'

'Out, damned spot! Out, I say!' Nora projected her voice as she wrung her hands.

'That which hath made them drunk hath made me bold,' Desmond said, up and out of his seat once more, flailing an arm theatrically. 'What hath quenched them hath given me fire.'

'Fair is foul, and foul is fair,' Nora said, continuing to pluck random lines from the play to throw at her opponent.

'Knock, knock, knock!' Desmond rapped on the table. 'Who's there, in the name of Beelzebub?'

'There's daggers in men's smiles,' Nora said. Neither were making any sense, but both refused to concede defeat by being the first to miss coming back with a quote.

Elspeth, having had enough of such nonsense, attempted to return to her seat and distance herself from this faux intellectual exchange. Desmond threw up his arms in alarm as he stepped to block her path. 'Something wicked this way comes,' he said, pleased with himself for remembering a line with any relevance to the situation.

Elspeth stopped dead, pursed her lips and responded in a slow and measured manner, 'Blood will have blood.'

A collective gasp went up and Desmond was floored for a moment before he said, 'How now, you secret, black, and midnight hag!'

The accused hag narrowed her eyes, drawing in a deep

breath as she stepped right up in front of Desmond. Her voice low and menacing, she said, 'Double, double toil and trouble; fire burn and cauldron bubble. Cool it with a *baboon's* blood, then the charm is firm and good.' Her emphasis on baboon made it clear to whom she was referring.

Desmond stood, slack-jawed, unable to form a response – as stunned as the rest of us. Nora started a clap, which was soon picked up by everyone else in the room. Our resident rascal recovered and soon was beaming as he turned to allow Elspeth past, nodding in acknowledgement of a worthy opponent.

Elspeth tried her best to mask her pleasure, but there were limits to even her composure, a small smirk of delight escaping as she took her seat.

'Well, on that bombshell,' I said once the room had calmed down a little, 'that's all for tonight, folks. And I guess I'll be seeing you tomorrow bright and early for Desmond's mystery outing.'

With tonight's activity completed to everyone's satisfaction, the Sunset Villas' elderly residents packed up their personal dabbers and ambled out of the hall with the promise of tea, biscuits, and late-night news in the TV lounge.

Barry, my old mentor, paused a moment to give me a supportive thumbs up – always appreciated – then made his way out with the rest, his progress painfully slow.

Nora caught my eye with a wink and an air-kiss as I packed away the bingo balls. She was always good fun, but sometimes hard work too. I wouldn't have her any other way, but I had some low-level anxiety about what she might try tomorrow.

Then I noticed another of my favourites making her way towards my table as I finished up.

'I'm sorry I couldn't rig the game to get you that nice bottle of port,' I said, glad to have Gladys' more stereotypical grandmotherly presence after such a turbulent bingo night.

'Don't you worry about that, my boy,' she said, waving away the comment. 'I was just coming over to say how pleased I am that you've found someone special. We all are, and I'm sure your grandmother would have been too.'

'Oh, thanks Gladys,' I said, after a moment of trouble getting the words out. 'I'm... Yeah, I'm pretty excited —'

'And we appreciate your wish to have your privacy respected,' she said, steamrolling over what I had to say – not that I knew yet what it was I had to say. 'But, you see... we haven't got much time left, us oldies. We could drop off at any minute. I mean, I don't like to say it, but Barry is practically on death's door – you saw him tonight, I'm sure. You two spent a lot of time together when you were younger whenever you came to visit your Nana. Why, he's the one who got you into calling the bingo for us, and he's almost too frail to make it out of his room by himself anymore. Do you see?'

I sat in silence, astonished that Gladys could – or would! – guilt me so hard. Not the benign little old granny I'd always thought I'd known. She was really turning the screw here.

'There's no good holding anything back, my dear,' she said, continuing when she found me unresponsive. 'You wouldn't want to regret not including us – giving us the joy of young love – would you? You've been holding out on us for two weeks now. Every day counts when you get to our age.'

She was right. These people were some of my oldest – in both meanings of the word – friends. And I would be introducing them to someone who was becoming increasingly important to me, even over such a short period. I mean, we'd already committed to attending Richard and Lucy's wedding together – this was getting serious. It wasn't just that, though. My friends at the Sunset Villas retirement home would be expecting me to turn up with a lovely lady on my arm – all very old-fashioned and traditional. To be fair to them, I'd done nothing to disabuse them of that notion. And I didn't want to give them a heart attack turning up with Gabriel on my arm – gorgeous, but very much not a lady. I couldn't jeopardise my relationship with these people—

Here I went – again! – making excuses for myself. Coming out to my mates hadn't gone at all as I'd planned, but it had been so much better. Who's to say this won't be the same? And what had made me think coming out would be a one-time deal? I was quickly coming to realise it was an ongoing process, something I'd have to do over and over and over.

'Perhaps another time, Gladys,' I said, not mentally prepared to have this conversation right now.

I watched her wrinkled face fall.

'All right, dear.' She patted my hand before following the others out of the makeshift bingo hall.

I felt wretched, watching as the room emptied.

'Wimp,' I mumbled to myself.

Are you keen to find out what happens next?
Grab yourself a copy of *Over and Out*:
www.gbralph.com/over-and-out

Acknowledgements

Releasing *Duck and Dive* involved a huge number of firsts for me. I'd never put something I'd written out in public, then actually told people about it. I hadn't even told my friends or family about my writing until then. But as soon as they heard, they jumped in to help promote my novella through word of mouth, social media posts, and group chat gossip. Even though some in Drag Box were two bottles deep by that point in the evening.

It was heartwarming to receive such a positive and enthusiastic response. I am so grateful for this. I was overwhelmed with lovely messages and fantastic feedback on Amazon and Goodreads – for something I wrote! And I watched with wonder as my sales figures soared into double figures – heady stuff.

On the administrative front, I set up author profiles so my mother could follow me on Facebook, Goodreads, and Amazon. You can too, if you're so inclined? There's my more established (and not author-specific) Twitter and Instagram profiles too. They're all linked on my website: www.gbralph.com

It was daunting – the publishing process, and telling everyone about my writing – but it was great fun. And much like the content of the book, it felt as if I was coming out all over again. The book was up and people had not only bought it, but they'd read it, rated and reviewed it, told their friends and shared it on their social media. *Duck and*

Dive was even mentioned on a bookish podcast (what!).

I did it – the end, right?

I thought so. Then a bunch of readers said they were looking forward to seeing what happened next. My first reaction was that there was no 'next' – the end of *Duck and Dive* was where we left the characters. That's all folks. But now I had the thought in my head... Well, just as the characters had amused me so much that their tale grew from a mere short story into a novella, I was soon humming with ideas about where they might go next.

Now, while the Covid-19 lockdown had a massive impact on the world, my partner and I were fortunate to remain employed and in good health during this time. Outside my day job's work hours, the occasional grocery shop and our daily lap around the park, I had plenty of time to prepare and publish *Duck and Dive*. And then – still in lockdown – I thought I might as well get stuck into the next part of the story.

So, on a bleak Saturday morning – two weeks after publishing *Duck and Dive* – I started the first draft of *Slip and Slide*. With a rough outline and ideas for a few key events along the way, I thought I'd see how the story developed from there.

I want to thank my partner – Te Peeti – and our flatmates – Mike and Michelle – for putting up with me while locked in the house together full-time for three months. They didn't begrudge me for taking over half the dining table all day and all evening. And they checked in often to make sure the cats made ample appearances in the book.

On that note, I must thank the neighbours' cats – Buddha, Snowball, and Barclay – for their exceptional work every day in keeping us sane during lockdown. Though, I like to think it was a mutually beneficial arrangement. We provided them a safe haven from the neighbours' dog – Agnes – and young children – names unknown. We regularly replenished their water bowl and provided an abundance of napping spots. In return, they accepted our pats, did amusing things, and were all-round adorable.

Te Peeti deserves thanks for the many culinary queries which he answered thoroughly and with patience during the first draft. And then after many rounds of edits, I subjected him once again to being the first to read my work. Despite the typo on the first page – which I blame on the third round of edits – he finished it. And his input made the book that much better.

To Alex and her assistant, Leon, thank you for your feedback. Apologies for the lack of bingo chat, but I'm glad you enjoyed the cat content. Thank you for exposing my occasional changes in tense, narrative perspective, typos, and clunky sentences. Also, thank you for your supportive and enthusiastic comments – they made editing for the fifth or sixth time a pleasure. I'm looking forward to taking you to Arthur's cafe for brunch.

Cam, thank you for your eagle-eyed typo hunting skills – they've added that extra layer of polish. I will never understand how you can read so quickly and so thoroughly, especially when you're supposed to be moving house and unpacking boxes.

Thank you to my Facebook and Twitter followers who responded to my survey about potential book cover designs. One design dominated, with a few calls for elements from the other options to be incorporated too. And that's exactly what I did. The modified design is what I've put on the cover, and it's so much better for everyone's feedback.

Now, the final product came in at approximately 35,000 words, which is 60% longer than *Duck and Dive*. So, I want to say a huge thanks to you for reading all this way. I hope you enjoyed hearing Gabriel's side of the story and are keen to see what's in store for him and Arthur next.

Printed in the USA
CPSIA information can be obtained
at www.ICGtesting.com
LVHW041546030924
789802LV00063B/664

9 780473 590727